ROAD SIGNS THAT SAY WEST

ROAD SIGNS

THAT

SAY

WEST

Sylvia Gunnery

pajamapress

www.pajamapress.ca   info@pajamapress.ca

 Canada Council Conseil des arts
for the Arts du Canada

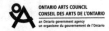 ONTARIO ARTS COUNCIL
CONSEIL DES ARTS DE L'ONTARIO
an Ontario government agency
un organisme du gouvernement de l'Ontario

 Canadä

The publisher gratefully acknowledges the support of the Canada Council for the Arts and the Ontario Arts Council for its publishing program. We acknowledge the financial support of the Government of Canada through the Canada Book Fund (CBF) for our publishing activities.

Library and Archives Canada Cataloguing in Publication

Gunnery, Sylvia, author
    Road signs that say west / Sylvia Gunnery.

ISBN 978-1-77278-023-9 (softcover)

    I. Title.

PS8563.U575R59 2017   jC813'.54   C2016-907866-3

Publisher Cataloging-in-Publication Data (U.S.)

Names: Gunnery, Sylvia, author.
Title: Road Signs That Say West / Sylvia Gunnery.
Description: Toronto, Ontario Canada : Pajama Press, 2017. | Summary: "Left to house-sit one summer while their parents are in Europe, three sisters set out on a cross-country road trip instead. Through near disasters, new acquaintances, and the revelation of close-kept secrets, the sisters' ties are by turns tested and strengthened"— Provided by publisher.
Identifiers: ISBN 978-1-77278-023-9 (paperback)
Subjects: LCSH: Sisters – Fiction. | Suicide -- Fiction. | Depressed persons -- Fiction. | Sexual abuse victims – Fiction. | BISAC: YOUNG ADULT FICTION / Family / Siblings.
Classification: LCC PZ7.G866Roa |DDC 813.6 – dc23

Cover design—Rebecca Buchanan
Interior design and typesetting—Rebecca Buchanan, and Martin Gould / martingould.com

Manufactured by Webcom
Printed in Canada

Pajama Press Inc.
181 Carlaw Ave. Suite 207 Toronto, Ontario Canada, M4M 2S1

Distributed in Canada by UTP Distribution
5201 Dufferin Street Toronto, Ontario Canada, M3H 5T8

Distributed in the U.S. by Ingram Publisher Services
1 Ingram Blvd. La Vergne, TN 37086, USA

For my sister Barb,

remembering our own summer road trip across Canada

Sometimes all we have are the lines on the road to guide us.
Sometimes all we have are the stars in the sky to shine their light.

Catherine MacLellan
"Lines on the Road"

PART ONE

Chapter One

"We'll do it. Everything you said."

"And all the contact numbers—"

"—Are on the fridge," says Hanna. "I put them there, just like you told me, Mom."

"The girls'll be fine, Marjorie. They know how to take care of themselves. Remember, we're the ones who brought them up. Here, one more round of hugs before takeoff."

"I know you'll be fine. Of course you will." Their mother hugs each of them—Hanna, Claire, and Megan—kissing their cheeks, then standing back for a final, tearful gaze. Each daughter has her own distinct features, though if you look closely, around their mouths, the way they smile, you'd definitely say they're sisters. Hanna is thin, maybe too thin, and probably a result of what she went through in Italy. Megan is tall, moving like any athlete, aware of her body more as a function of sport than as sensual. The deep red lipstick something new she's trying. And dear Claire, in the shadow of her older sisters, too critical of her weight compared to theirs, wishing she hadn't inherited her dad's curls when Hanna and Megan had silky long hair. "Look at the three of you," their mother says. "All grown up when it seems like only yesterday—"

"—We were crapping in our diapers."

"Hanna!"

"Come on, Marj, let's get through security before our tickets expire. Have fun, girls!" He catches the quick look in his wife's eyes. "Good, clean fun, of course."

"Bye, Dad. Bye, Mom. Bye! Bye! Bye!" They call and wave as their parents show their boarding passes and step into the security area. They keep waving as their mom drops her passport and bends to retrieve it. Their dad walks on ahead, pulling both small suitcases, and their mom turns to wave again.

The security doors slide shut.

"There. That's it," says Hanna. "Mom and Dad are off on their trip of a lifetime." She pulls the car keys out of her shorts pocket and jingles them like toy bells. "And so are we!" She turns and heads toward the exit.

Megan is right behind her. "What're you talking about?"

"So are we?" Claire stops scrolling through pictures she'd just taken.

"Listen," says Hanna in that authoritative voice only the oldest sister could pull off, "a house is a house, not a person. It doesn't need anyone to look after it." She keeps walking toward the exit. "What are we supposed to do that the alarm system can't?"

"We're supposed to do exactly what Mom and Dad told us to do. House-sit while they're in Europe." As usual, Megan attempts to be the voice of reason. As usual, it comes across as sarcasm wrapped in a thin gauze of disdain.

"What trip, Hanna?" asks Claire.

"A road trip from sea to sea." The automatic doors slide open and she walks out. "Atlantic to Pacific. Halifax to Vancouver."

"Are you insane?" Megan's voice is now up a few decibels. "Mom and Dad would never agree to this!"

"That's why she didn't ask," says Claire.

At fifteen, Claire has spent enough time observing her older sisters to recognize all the patterns. Hanna, though she's mostly a spur-of-the-moment type, always has the important details covered. Megan needs to hear everything out loud before it even starts to make sense—when she studies for tests, she mutters continuously to herself.

"I'm offering this amazing once-in-a-lifetime trip across Canada together. Everything paid by me."

Megan isn't impressed. "How long have you been planning this?"

"Since last night."

"Oh, great. You think we can just jump in the car and drive all the way to Vancouver and back again and be sitting on the couch watching TV when Mom and Dad get home?"

"Yeah. Something like that." Hanna stops at the ticket station to pay for parking. "Anyone got some change?"

Claire reaches past Hanna and puts a coin into the slot.

"I'm not going," says Megan. "I just started my job and there's only two months before university starts in the fall."

"That lame job doesn't pay enough. You'll have to get a student loan anyway. Besides, you must know what you look like in a hairnet."

"At least I'm serious about university. I don't plan on dropping out."

Hanna lets that go.

Claire is already imagining them on the prairie, golden fields on both sides of the highway and, off in the distance, a long train carving a dark line across the horizon. "When are we leaving?"

"Today."

They back out of the driveway, the air-conditioning struggling against the July heat and the trunk crammed with backpacks, sleeping bags, air mattresses, pillows, and the old tent they used to put up in their yard when they were kids. Claire is sharing the backseat with Hanna's guitar in its soft case.

Megan has taken over from their mother as family interrogator. Hanna has the right answer every time. Yes, the alarm system is set; yes, perishables are thrown out; yes, the newspaper is canceled; and yes, the answering machine has a new message: *Hi, this is Hanna, Megan, and Claire. We're home alone, hiding under the bed in terror while a snarling dog and a shadowy figure with a flashlight prowl around outside. Leave a message and your number. We'll get back to you...if we can.*

"What did Mrs. MacAuley say when you asked if she'd get our mail out of the box?" asks Megan. "I know for sure Mom would've told her to keep an eye on us."

"She said she was surprised—shocked—that Mom decided we should stay with cousins in Cape Breton and she hadn't realized we had Cape Breton relatives and did we know any of the Baddeck MacAuleys and would we take a meat pie to her brother who works on the locks at the Canso Causeway."

"Where's the pie?" asks Claire.

"She's likely still trying to find it at the bottom of her freezer. How could I take that pie? She'd be calling her brother to make sure he got it, and her next call would be to the police."

"Because of a missing meat pie?"

"No, Megan, not because of a missing meat pie."

"Anyone want some cake?" Claire picks up the plastic container from the floor beside her feet and takes the lid off.

"Hey! My birthday cake!" says Hanna. "First stop—coffee."

Megan turns around and looks in the container. "You brought leftover birthday cake? Seriously?"

"Why not? It's only three days old," says Claire. "There's still a rose left. Anyone want the rose?"

"You have it," says Hanna. "A reward for bringing the cake."

"I don't believe this. You two are acting like we're taking an ordinary drive around the block and back home again."

"It is ordinary," says Hanna. "People do this all the time. They just get in their cars and follow road signs that say west. What's the problem?"

"You're nineteen, Hanna. Nineteen! Mom and Dad put us, but mostly you, in charge of the house, and what are we doing? We're abandoning our house, lying to the neighbors, stealing Mom's car—"

"Oh, give it up, Megan. Stealing Mom's car. That's so hyper-exaggerated. She said we could use her car and we're using it."

"Practically stealing Mom's car and driving all the way across Canada when Mom and Dad think we're home. I'm so stupid for letting you talk me into quitting my job."

"Think hairnet and thank me."

"Check this." Claire leans forward to show Megan. "First photo of our road trip. You guys arguing—I mean discussing."

Hanna pulls into the drive-thru and orders three espressos on ice.

"I'm not eating stale cake," says Megan. "And delete that picture right now. I look like a criminal."

Rain starts before they get to Truro, a few fat drops splatting against the windshield.

"Hey! Glooscap!" says Claire. "Let's stop and get a picture. Day one of the Three Sisters' Road Trip!"

"In the rain?" says Megan.

"It's not raining much."

Hanna is already signaling to turn off at the exit.

"You won't get the whole statue in the picture," mutters Megan.

"Smile!" says Claire.

By the time they cross the border into New Brunswick two hours later, it's a downpour.

Hanna starts singing "Farewell to Nova Scotia" and Claire joins in: *"For when I am far away on the briny ocean tossed..."*

Megan crosses her arms, looks out the window, frowns at the miserable day, and sighs.

"Will you ever heave a sigh and a wish for me?"

"Will youuu e-ver heave a sigh-igh and a wish forrrr meeeee?"

The windshield wipers slam back and forth, a monotonous rhythm competing with the music on the radio or their random conversations, one of which is about staying at a motel instead of camping.

"No wimping out on our first night," says Claire.

"Check for campgrounds near Edmundston, then," says Hanna.

"Here's one. It's by a river that goes under a bridge, and there's a waterfall. They've even got volleyball and tennis."

"Like who cares?" says Megan. "It's raining."

"And a heated swimming pool."

"We'll stop and eat before we get there," says Hanna.

Claire's phone chimes.

It's Matt. *Where r u?*

She texts back. *Edmundston almost.*

Going 2 lake aftr work.

Alone?

It'll be ok. Don't worry.

When almost everyone else who knew Caleb avoids even saying his name, Matt still counts him as his best friend. In a way, it makes sense to go to the lake, Caleb's favorite place. Matt will do whatever he wants anyway. And he'll probably be okay.

The parking lot beside the campground registration office is partially flooded and it's still raining. Hanna is soaked when she gets back in the car. "We're number 25." She hands Megan the campground map. "It's near the swimming pool."

"I love tenting in the rain," says Claire. "The sound it makes on the tent. The cozy feeling being all warm in my sleeping bag."

"In your squishy, wet sleeping bag," says Megan. "That old tent will probably leak." She looks at the small map. "Number 25 should be...there it is. Let's wait and see if the rain stops."

"It's not stopping. I just checked the radar," says Claire. "I'm putting on my bathing suit. Pop the trunk, Hanna. You guys want your backpacks?"

They squirm into their bathing suits, slinking down in the car, though their chances of being seen are nil. Everyone at the campground is inside the few vulnerable tents pitched nearby or their tightly shut RVs.

By the time their tent is up and the sleeping bags, pillows, and Hanna's guitar are tucked inside, the mood turns zany. Who cares if people peer at them from RV windows or poke their heads out through tent flaps?

Claire runs to the pool and does a cannonball. Before she surfaces, Hanna is right beside her.

"I feel like a little kid!" yells Claire.

"You are a little kid!" Hanna ducks down, grabs Claire's legs, and pulls her under.

Megan does a perfect dive and swims to the other end of the pool. Strong, expert strokes. Fast, as if she's competing.

Claire lies back and floats, her arms spread wide, her face spattered with rain. Heavy drops hit the water and splash up, creating tiny craters around her. "I love this, Hanna."

"Me too."

"I'm glad you're not in Italy anymore."

"Me too."

Soon, their bikinis and towels are in a wet clump outside the tent and they're cozy inside. Evening light seeps through the walls.

Hanna plays her guitar, imitating the sound of rain, mostly high notes trickling down to a few heavy drops of low ones. She hums softly. Every so often, she stops and jots something in her notebook.

"Megan, scrunch over by Hanna so I can take a picture to send Mom and Dad."

"Don't forget Dad's minimum-contact rule," says Hanna. "So Mom won't get heart palpitations if she doesn't hear from us every day. And maybe they shouldn't know where we are yet, anyway."

"I'll just say we're camping in our backyard like when we were little. That'll get them all nostalgic."

"And delusional," says Megan.

Chapter Two

The rain has stopped. Hanna and Megan are still awake, but Claire is asleep between them.

Megan feels the outside of her sleeping bag. "It's a miracle," she whispers. "My sleeping bag's dry. Can't believe this old tent doesn't leak."

Hanna flips her pillow over and settles back down. "And don't worry. Mom and Dad'll be okay with this when we tell them."

"Hanna?"

"Mm?"

"How come you came home from Italy?"

"Stuff happened."

"Why's it like this big secret?"

"It really wasn't anything."

"Now you're lying. I hate when people lie."

"Things got blown out of proportion."

"I know you and Mom and Dad went to a lawyer."

"They wanted a letter sent to make sure…"

"To make sure what? Tell me."

"Okay, okay. Here's what happened." Hanna leans up on one elbow, her voice still low. "I got fired. *Dismissed*, they called it. I was planning on quitting anyway. The only reason they wanted an au pair was so they could forget they actually had a five-year-old kid."

"But why fire you?"

"Mrs. Gallo accused me of having a thing going with her husband."

"That's insane!"

"Shhhh. You'll wake up Claire."

"Where'd she get off thinking that?"

"Someone said they saw something they didn't actually see. She started sending me all these threats. Even after I left, she still texted stuff. So Mom and Dad got a lawyer to send a letter and make her stop."

"But Mr. Gallo knew there was nothing going on. He could've done something."

"He apologized. When I left, he gave me money."

"That's how you're paying for this trip."

"Partly."

Megan is quiet for a moment. "You haven't been using your phone. It's because of those threats, isn't it?"

"It's no big deal." She snuggles down into her sleeping bag. "Let's get some sleep. If we head out real early tomorrow, we can make it to Montreal. There's a dance club on St. Catherine Street I want us to go to."

"You're the only one with ID."

"We'll figure something out."

"You'll get us in trouble."

"Night, Megan."

Snow had started before dawn, drifting lightly down, coating everything with white, and gradually building into deep, soft mounds. School was canceled. Caleb might have fallen back to sleep before his parents left for work.

He couldn't have slept for long. By ten, he would have been at least halfway to the lake. He probably drove slowly, not because of his father's old truck with its unreliable tires, but because of the feeling he must have had, knowing where he was going and why. On the 101, there would've been a lot of traffic despite the snowfall warnings—people late for work, inching along, knowing the commute home would be even worse. The truck radio wasn't on.

He stopped at the cabin, got the key out of the wood box on the veranda, and went inside. How much time he spent inside is not clear. He didn't start a fire in the wood stove. Any footprints that could have marked his path into the cabin or around it would soon be deep under snow.

In the stillness, snow fell and fell and fell.

A breeze began. Snowflakes, some as large as moths, twirled and skidded in the air, gray against the gray sky and white against the deep green of spruce and pine trees. Branches gradually bowed low under the weight of snow.

At some point, Caleb got back into the truck and drove to the very end of the road, where people who didn't own property on the lake launched their boats or parked cars to go swimming or skating. Was the snow deep when he stepped out of the truck? Did he have to kick drifts away so he could get down on his knees and reach the tailpipe? Did he brush off his jeans before he got back in the truck and turned on the ignition?

The phone call from Matt that night had been terrifying.

Not far outside Edmundston, they cross from New Brunswick into Quebec and decide they'll stop in Rivière-du-Loup for a late breakfast.

"If we go down the 132 on this side of the St. Lawrence," says Claire, "and then take the 134, we'll cross at the Jacques Cartier Bridge. Montreal's about four-and-a-half hours from Rivière-du-Loup, not counting any stops. The hostel's on Rue Saint-Denis."

"As long as it's not far from St. Catherine Street," says Hanna.

"As long as it's not a dump," says Megan.

"It says it's the newest hostel in Montreal. The pictures look pretty good. We could get a room for four people and maybe no one'll take the extra bunk. And let's see...there's St. Catherine Street. A couple of blocks south."

The small room has bunk beds on opposite sides of a window that looks out on a miniscule backyard. A narrow dirt lane, barely wide enough for a single car, is next to the yard.

On one of the bottom bunks are dark-rimmed glasses, a bag of jujubes, a scarf, a book, and a hairbrush. Two mustard-yellow sneakers with red laces are upside down on the floor.

"Looks like we have a roommate," says Hanna.

"Cool sneakers," says Claire.

"I'm taking a top bunk," says Megan. "No way I'm looking over at some stranger when I wake up."

"I'm gonna go put my guitar in the locker. Be right back."

Claire climbs the ladder and stretches out on the bunk. "This is pretty comfortable."

"Bonjour!" A tall, large girl with a tangle of curly red hair bursts into the room carrying two oversized shopping bags. She's wearing a short plaid skirt and a yellow T-shirt that says: *I'm listening. I'm just not paying attention.* When she walks across the room, her flip-flops make a slapping sound. "Quan at the front desk said you guys were here. Sisters, *n'est pas?* I'm Gina...Jackie. *Voila!* My glasses! Thought I left them on the metro." She plops the shopping bags next to her bunk. "My bladder's screaming. *Excusez-moi.*" The bathroom door shuts behind her.

Megan looks up at Claire with an exaggerated frown. Claire shrugs.

Hanna comes into the room and sees the shopping bags. "Our roommate?"

"Gina," says Megan.

"Jackie," says Claire.

"Huh?"

They hear water running in the sink. The toilet flushes and the girl reappears.

"Hi. I'm Hanna."

"I'm Jackie."

"First you said you were Gina," says Megan with a distinct ping of criticism.

"Changed my name. As of yesterday, whatever's connected to my parents doesn't exist." She gathers her long hair into a manageable wad and ties it at the back. "Except for Willie. I'll sneak home to see him. Even next year when I finish high school and probably move somewhere else, Toronto maybe, I'll still come back to see him."

"Is he your brother?" asks Claire.

"Mon *chien*."

Claire catches Megan's *whatever* look. "Willie's a fun name for a dog," she says.

"So, what's up with *les trois soeurs* in Montreal?"

"We're on a road trip," says Hanna. "Halifax to Vancouver."

"Cool."

"Montreal's our first main stop. We're going to Metropolis tonight."

"You won't get in without ID. I can get you in a place I know of if you guys wanna come with me and Adele."

Seven hours later, Hanna and Claire are waiting in the emergency department of St. Mary's Hospital while Megan's wrist is being X-rayed. "I fell," was all she would say to the admissions nurse.

Hanna flips through another magazine, then tosses it back on the table.

"Those guys who lifted Jackie and Adele up must've thought Megan wanted to crowd surf, too," says Claire.

"Likely would've been okay if she just went with it."

"If her arm's broken, do we have to go home?"

"I don't know. Probably not." Hanna picks up another magazine, but doesn't open it. "We can just pay whatever it costs and she can make some kind of medical claim when she gets back home."

The door to the examination area opens and everyone in the waiting room looks up. A man hobbles out on crutches.

"I wasn't asleep last night," says Claire. "When you guys were talking about why you came home from Italy."

Hanna leans back in her chair and rests her head against the wall. Then she looks at Claire. "I didn't tell Megan everything last night."

The door opens again and Megan comes out. Her right arm is in a sling and her wrist is wrapped in bandaging. She looks exhausted.

"What's the verdict?" says Hanna, trying a half-cheerful smile. She takes the pamphlet Megan is holding.

"My wrist is sprained. I have to keep it up like this for a couple of days and put ice on it. And not move it much. We have to get painkillers. The regular kind, not prescription."

"At least it's not your right wrist," says Claire.

Megan gives Claire a look. "Hanna, you have to fill out some papers. You're the adult. As if. But anyway."

"It says here you have to see a doctor before you stop wearing the bandage and sling. What doctor? Where?"

"Don't ask me. And don't act like this is my fault, either. It wasn't my idea—"

"Okay, okay. Let's just fill out those papers and get back to the hostel."

"You probably think I did this on purpose to ruin the trip."

"No, Megan. I don't think that." Hanna goes to the admissions desk.

"The trip's not ruined," says Claire. "We don't have to go back home."

"This is painful. Very painful. I feel like my wrist's blown up like a balloon and there's sharp needles pushing right into my bones. The very last thing I want is to sit for hours and hours in that car with this." She lifts her sling, and winces.

"It'd be the same if we went home," says Claire. "You'd still have to be in the car for a couple of days. May as well be—"

"Don't talk to me." Megan gently rubs her bandaged wrist as if it's an injured kitten.

"We're good to go," says Hanna. "She said you should get your wrist checked tomorrow at a walk-in clinic to make sure the swelling goes down like it's supposed to. She wrote the address on this pamphlet."

Megan's already walking ahead of them toward the exit.

"It was still fun," says Claire. "I mean, before Megan got hurt."

"The band was super amazing."

"That was my first-ever dance bar. I'll pretty much remember it for the rest of my life."

Chapter Three

Claire and Hanna are sitting under a tree in a park not far from the hostel. The tent is spread out on the grass to dry. Megan has gone for a walk, griping about how the wrist injury is messing up her running routine.

"Last night you said you didn't tell Megan everything about what happened in Italy. Tell me what you didn't you tell her."

"It wasn't like I was not telling her. Not on purpose."

"Maybe the guy cheats on his wife all the time and so she thought he was cheating with you."

"Sex complicates everything."

"You had sex with him!"

"I didn't say that. Don't jump to conclusions."

"He's married! He's a father! And he's ancient!"

"If you're going to keep yelling, Claire, we're not having this conversation. And thirty-two isn't ancient."

"Tell me what you didn't tell Megan."

Hanna looks up through the branches. Leafy patterns dapple her face. "There's not much to tell. Not really. It's confusing. I don't know."

"You sound like you had the hots for him."

"You're jumping to conclusions again. The only time he even talked to me when no one else was around was after I got fired and he gave me the money. I'm positive he didn't want Mrs. Gallo to know about that money."

"Okay. I get it. Nothing really happened and then you got fired. You didn't like that job anyway. Why think about it, Hanna? It's not worth it."

"So I should take my little sister's advice and just let it go, right?"

"Right."

Hanna closes her eyes and leans back against the tree. If letting go was only that simple.

At the Edmundston campground, long after Megan had gone back to sleep, Hanna crept very quietly out of their tent. The rain had stopped, but the grass was wet on her bare feet. She walked to the river where the small waterfall rushed and tumbled. Her phone was in her hand, still turned off. The phone was the reason she was standing out there in the darkness by herself.

The threats had not stopped. There were two on Wednesday. Then, before they left Halifax yesterday, this text:

You run to your mommy and daddy, do you? This is the biggest joke. They do not know their daughter. I say to them and to everyone who Hanna is. A liar. A husband thief. A teenager bitch!

Just thinking of that text made her cringe. It was like, if Mrs. Gallo kept saying this stuff all the time, people would eventually end up believing it was true.

It was so stupid!

Hanna raised her arm, leaned back, and threw her phone into the river. She watched the current swirl at the bottom of the waterfall, circles of foam spinning away.

Claire walks over to the tent, lifts one corner, and gives it a shake. "I think if we pitched this it'd dry faster."

"It'll be okay. We'll pitch it tomorrow when we get to Ottawa."

Claire goes back to the shade and sits down. She's thinking about the way Hanna just said, *It's confusing.* "I had a dream about Caleb the other night. It was about when he died."

"Wanna tell me about it?"

"I don't know." Claire brushes her fingers lightly over the grass, watching the blades bend and spring back up.

For a moment, Hanna thinks she's not going to say anything.

"In the dream, it's snowing real hard. First, he's in his father's truck and then he gets to the lake. It's like I'm there. I can see everything. The cabin, snow, trees. Everything.

Then it's like I'm squeezing my eyes shut so I can't see any more."

Hanna reaches over and touches her arm. "Oh, Claire."

"When Matt called me that night, I could hear his mother saying something. She was right there beside him. Like he couldn't be alone when he told me what happened. He was really scared. I knew as soon as he said my name."

"It's really sad. Really, really sad."

"I keep thinking if school wasn't canceled, he would've been with us. Maybe he would've said something."

"Thinking about *what if* is impossible when something already happened. It just hurts you more."

Claire looks out across the park and sees Megan walking along the path, keeping her crowd-surfing wrist up like the nurse told her to. "Here comes Megan."

They watch her cut across the grass toward them.

"Don't tell her about my dream, okay?"

"I won't."

As she gets closer, they can see she's in a bad mood. "I need to go back to the hostel. This is throbbing."

"We have to go to that walk-in clinic soon, anyway." Hanna puts her guitar in its case, then helps Claire roll up the tent and stuff it in the bag.

As they walk across the park to the car, Megan stays ahead of them. Claire is pretty sure she's thinking about all the things she shouldn't have done, like quit her job and come on this road trip.

Jackie's bed has been stripped and the blanket folded

with the pillow on top. The two large shopping bags are packed beside the bunk.

"Moving day," says Hanna.

Megan kicks off her sneakers and climbs awkwardly up to her bunk.

"Hey! *Bonjour*, you guys!" Jackie walks in, folding money into a small pink change purse. "Looks like you got fixed up." She's still wearing the clothes she had on last night.

"Her wrist's just sprained," says Claire.

"Lucky. I knew this girl who got dropped crowd surfing. Actually dropped, not just accidentally falling with people trying to catch you. She cracked a lot of bones in her arm and had to have two major operations. *Deux!*"

Megan hasn't even lifted her head off the pillow. Her eyes are closed.

"You leaving?" Hanna doesn't mean it to sound the way it does, like *hurry up and get out*. She isn't blaming Jackie for what happened. Not really.

"I'm moving in with Adele at her parents' place." She looks down at the two shopping bags. "So anyway...well, you guys have a fun trip."

"Thanks," says Claire. "Hope you get to see Willie a lot."

"Certainement!" Jackie grins and picks up the bags. *"Au revoir, mes amis!"*

The door shuts loudly behind her.

"Hope you get to see Willie a lot? Like who cares?" says Megan. "This is a person who made me practically break my wrist."

"She—" But Claire stops. Why argue?

"Have a little nap, Megan," says Hanna, gently. "Then we'll go to that clinic. Sure you don't want a painkiller?"

"I'm positive. You can get addicted to those things."

"It's basically just aspirin."

"Extra-strength," says Megan, to prove a point.

Claire climbs up to her bunk. Since Matt's message about going to the lake, she hasn't heard from him, though she texted a couple of times. Not that he texted every second of every day, but he'd usually at least be asking what's up. She reads a few pages of her book but can't concentrate. "I'm just going outside. It's too warm in here."

In the backyard, on the small patch of lawn under a tree, is a picnic table painted purple with wildly colored flowers all over the top. No one else is in the yard. She sits at the picnic table and phones Matt. He doesn't answer and she doesn't leave a message. She tries his house and his mother answers.

"This is Claire, Mrs. Ryan. Is Matt home?" There is a slight hesitation that makes her hold her breath.

"Matt's with his father right now. They're visiting Caleb's parents. It's.... Has Matt been in touch with you? I know you're on a trip with your sisters."

"He texted me Friday. Said he was going to the lake."

"Yes, well.... He's been having some difficulties, dear. We didn't know he'd gone to the lake on Friday. Or that he didn't have a driver with him. When he wasn't home for supper—and that isn't like him because he knew his grandmother was coming—well, we were frantic with worry. The police found him. He'd been drinking and had fallen asleep in the car where Caleb.... Really, Claire, there's still so much sadness."

Claire could picture exactly where Matt would have been when the police found him. It was probably pelting rain by the time he left work on Friday. Maybe he went to the cabin first and didn't drive down to the end of the road until it got dark. What he'd done—drinking by himself and passing out like that—gave her a sick feeling.

"We think he'll be fine. He just has to get through this and...I don't know. He said he wanted to visit Caleb's parents, which he's been doing quite a lot. I think it's a comfort to them and to Matthew, too. Today his father went with him, to be there in a supportive way."

"Would you tell Matt I called, please? But he doesn't need to call me back or text or anything."

"He'll be seeing a counselor starting tomorrow. Maybe after a few sessions with the counselor, Matthew will be ready to be in touch with his friends again. I'm sure he'll be happy to know you called."

"Thanks, Mrs. Ryan."

"And, Claire?"

"Yes?"

"How are you doing, dear? Caleb was your close friend too."

"Not close like Matt was. But..." She doesn't like how she's measuring her friendship with Caleb. "I'm okay, Mrs. Ryan."

"It must be wonderful to be on a trip with your sisters. This is the time to do those things. While you're young."

"Yeah. Well...thanks, Mrs. Ryan. Tell Matt I hope he's okay."

"I will. Have a safe journey, dear."

She sits at the picnic table, looking down at the painted flowers. White daisies and purple coneflowers and broad yellow petals of black-eyed Susans—all flowers they had in the garden back home. When they were kids, their mom taught them the names of flowers and how to distinguish weeds from the early growth of perennials. Whoever painted this table must have a garden.

"Claire! You coming with us?" Hanna is standing in the narrow lane beside the yard. "It's okay if you want to stay here."

"No. I'll come."

Megan is already in the car.

"After the clinic, we could walk up Saint Denis Street and go to one of those outside cafes," says Hanna cheerfully, trying to keep things from drowning.

"That'd be fun," says Claire.

"Whatever," says Megan.

Chapter Four

They hear music as they start down the hill, but it isn't until they're at the end of the lane that they realize it's coming from the backyard of the hostel. Someone has a rain stick, the cascading sound of rain so strange on this clear, full moon night.

"Let's check it out," says Hanna.

A guy playing guitar and singing is sitting on the picnic table with his feet on the seat. Beside him is a girl with a rain stick, and a bongo player is sitting on an overturned plastic bucket. A couple more people are on camp chairs, including Quan, the Vietnamese guy from the registration desk.

"Welcome, lovelies!" he says. "Join in! Please have beer!" He lightly kicks against the case of beer on the grass beside him and a couple of bottles clink.

"Okay," says Hanna. "Thanks."

"And for you," he says to Claire and Megan.

"You guys can have a beer if you want," says Hanna. "It's all right."

"I'll pass," says Megan.

"Me too. But thanks." Claire smiles at Quan and sits at the picnic table.

"Get your guitar," he says to Hanna. "Play your music for our little party."

"Sure." She puts her beer down beside Claire and goes inside.

A guy wearing a black T-shirt and knee-length brown shorts gets up from a camp chair. "You can sit here," he says to Megan. Is his accent Jamaican?

"I'm okay."

"What happened to your arm?"

Megan looks down at the sling. "I fell. It's just sprained. It doesn't hurt."

Claire can tell Megan likes this guy. Mostly from her eyes. And the way she talks. Softly. No attitude around the edges of her words.

"I'm Tajey," he says. He's tall. Athletic. Tight black corn-rows curve across his head and join in a small cluster at the back of his neck. His soft mustache is almost transparent against his brown skin.

Hanna comes back with her guitar. "I can't really play like you guys. You must be a band." She takes a long drink of beer.

"We're buskers. Street Muse," says the guy on the table.

"I'm Dennis. That's Paul there on bongos. And Rudy. This is Solange. She plays a mean rain stick."

Solange laughs and tilts the stick to make a soft trickle of rain slide through. "You don't exactly play this thing."

"Let us hear your lovely tunes," says Quan.

Someone leaves to get more beer.

Claire's phone vibrates. It's a text from their dad: *Great tenting pic. Is that really you there, Megan? LOL Here's Mom at Globe Theatre. London is hot, crowded, and expensive. Also fun, exciting, and old. Love you all. Cheerio.*

She sends a quick message back, feeling weird about everything she has to leave out.

Still nothing from Matt. She hasn't told Rachel or Cassie or anyone else what's going on with him right now. *Having some difficulties.* For five months, he pretty much kept things together. Stayed normal. Maybe this is the real normal.

She decides to go inside and read. Just be alone for a while.

Through the open window, she can hear Hanna and Dennis singing. He knows the song better than she does, but she's doing great harmonies. Claire has a sudden proud feeling listening to Hanna. She could always really sing.

When Claire wakes, she doesn't have a sense of how long she'd slept. Paul is still playing bongos, just slow and lazy. She leans over the side of the bunk and pushes the curtain back. Quan isn't there anymore. Neither are Solange and Dennis. Hanna and Ryan and another guy are sitting in camp chairs drinking beer, their feet up on the seat of the picnic table. Where are Megan and Tajey?

The next time Claire wakes up, Hanna is asleep but Megan's not around. Before she has a chance to think about where Megan could be, the door slowly opens and she comes in.

"Where were you?" Claire whispers.

"Walking."

"With that guy."

"Tajey."

"He's hot."

"He's really nice." Megan goes into the bathroom and carefully closes the door. She's in her pajamas when she comes back out. "Help me tie this."

Claire climbs quietly down from her bunk. "So tell me."

"Tell you what?"

"I know you've got the hots for him." She ties the sling and smoothes it around Megan's elbow.

"Think about it." There's Megan's familiar sarcasm again. "Tomorrow he takes a train home to New York and we go to Ottawa. It's not like I'll ever see him again."

"Who knows?"

"I know." She adjusts her arm in the sling. "Look. He's hot. He's nice. We went for a walk. That's it."

Early morning sun shines through the curtains. Hanna is still asleep and Megan is standing by the door. Her hair is in a ponytail, and she's wearing her red-striped camisole, pale blue tights, and no sling.

"Where're you going?" says Claire.

"Shhh." Megan glances toward Hanna. "I just want to say good-bye to Tajey." She softly closes the door behind her.

Claire tries to remember if Megan ever fell for a guy this fast before. She had lots of chances to. Guys sure fell for her. Instantly, because of her looks. Her height. The way she lifts her long, brown hair with the back of her hand and lets it fall behind her shoulder. But with Megan it's always like she can decide any minute whether to stop liking someone and start liking someone else. A light switch. Off. On. Off. Controlled.

Hanna snores softly. Claire wonders what she thought last night when Megan and Tajey left the backyard together. For sure, Megan wouldn't have looked in her direction.

Two backpacks are beside the door, ready to go. Hanna rubs her forehead to ease a small headache. She glances out and sees Claire at the picnic table. Megan's bed has been slept in. At least she came home last night. Maybe she's gone for a walk with that guy again. Tajey.

With Ottawa only a couple of hours away, they decide to go down to Old Montreal. Have lunch. Walk around. Do the tourist thing.

In a narrow street off Place Jacques Cartier, Megan stops in front of the window of a small jewelry store. "Think I'll get something. A souvenir of Montreal."

Hanna and Claire are both thinking the souvenir will be more about Tajey than about Montreal. She chooses earrings, thin wooden hoops, each with a small silver bird dangling inside.

Thunder rumbles as they find their way out of Montreal and onto the Trans-Canada Highway. Soon, the clouds soften and the sun comes out.

"Here's a campground we could stay at in Ottawa," says Claire, scrolling through the website. "Fifteen minutes from the Parliament Buildings. And there's a pool."

"Be nice to have a swim," says Hanna. Then she looks at Megan. "You could at least wade in the water. That won't hurt your wrist."

When their tent is pitched, with the flap wide open, it's still hot even though it's past eight. From their campsite, they can see the pool where kids are screaming and splashing.

"Kids never get out of pools when they have to pee," says Megan. "Gross."

Hanna grabs a towel and her backpack. "Let's just get showers and stay here tonight. We can go downtown tomorrow. I'm really tired."

"Why're you so tired?" says Megan. "It's not like we drove that far today."

"Meaning?"

"Nothing."

Claire looks from one sister to the other. What was that all about?

It's dark when the camper van arrives. Two bright beams slice across the picnic table where Megan and Claire are sitting. The van parks a couple of sites away, its lights still on. Five people get out, four guys and a girl.

In the quiet, Megan and Claire can hear every word they say.

"This'll work."

"I'm wacked. Brutal drive."

"Good place for your tent right over there, Al."

"Yeah."

"Where are the showers? I stink." This in the girl's voice.

A guy gets back in the van and turns it around. He leans out the window as another guy directs him. "Okay. Back. Back. Straighten up. Go ahead a bit and swing it left. Okay. Good. Back up. Keep comin'. Stop. That's it."

"Think I'll brush my teeth and go to bed," says Megan.

"I'll walk over to the washroom with you." Claire picks up the flashlight.

A Canadian flag towel is draped over the door of a shower stall. Steam wafts out. A bar of soap drops and spins across the cement floor. "Bloody hell."

"Got it," says Claire. Specks of grit coat one side. She puts the soap into the hand reaching beneath the shower door.

"Thanks!" Then, "Do they ever clean these floors? Gross."

Megan makes a face.

Claire reties Megan's sling, careful not to catch it on the silver-bird earrings. Souvenir of Tajey.

A girl with very short black hair comes out of the shower, wrapped in the flag towel. There's a lizard tattoo on her shoulder. "Hey, I think I saw you guys when we got here. Sitting at your table." She pulls clothes out of a large leather bag and starts to get dressed. "Where you from?"

"Halifax," says Claire.

"Cool. Maritimers. Us too. We're from Charlottetown. Well, Jerry's not, but he goes to UPEI with us. We're heading to North Bay for Jerry's sister's wedding."

"We're driving across Canada," says Claire. "With our other sister Hanna."

"Sounds fun."

"Yeah. It was Hanna's idea. We're supposed to be house-sitting while our parents are in Europe."

"The drive'll be way more fun." She pulls a hair dryer out of the bag.

"We have to go," says Megan, giving Claire a look.

"Probably see you tomorrow," says the girl.

As soon as they're outside, Megan says, "Do you have to tell everyone everything? Strangers don't need to know where we're from and what we're doing or where our parents are or anything."

"I bet you told Tajey plenty of stuff and you won't ever see him again in your life." She doesn't want to sound this mean, but it's so frustrating. The shell Megan wraps around herself. That mood always ready to bubble up and burst. "Did he even text you yet?"

Megan says nothing. She walks on ahead and goes into the tent.

Claire stays outside. A candle burns in the small jar they'd placed on the picnic table. She watches the flame bend and tremble, wishing it wasn't so easy to get mad at Megan.

She looks up at the stars. Millions and billions and trillions of stars. She starts to name the constellations. The Big Dipper. Obvious. And there's the Little Dipper with the North Star at the tip of the handle. Polaris. In fourth grade, they created the northern sky like a canopy above their desks. So many stars painted with florescent silver and dangling from fishing line so when the windows were covered with black paper and the lights were turned off, it was like they were inside the night universe.

And now, suddenly, she's thinking about Caleb again.

It was a clear, cold night, and a bunch of friends from their high school went sliding on Nixie's Hill. No one had toboggans or anything like that. They just had big pieces of cardboard and they'd go speeding and bumping down the hill, or tumbling and rolling off as the cardboard swirled away.

Caleb stayed at the top of the hill, hands deep in the pockets of his thick jacket, his hood falling over his eyes.

Claire, out of breath and salted with snow, dragged her cardboard the last few steps to the top. "Here. Want a turn?"

"Not up for it. Thanks though."

A couple of girls started down the hill on the same piece of cardboard. The one on back tipped and rolled off, then ran and skidded to catch the ride, laughing the whole time.

"It's fun," said Claire. A small wisp of breath drifted against her cheek.

"I know."

"You're real quiet. What's up?"

"Nothing. Not really." He pushed the hood off his face and looked up at the stars.

Claire looked up too.

"Don't you think sometimes when you look at stars," said Caleb, "and how big the sky is your eyes can't even see how big it is with all those stars, it's like you're just this insignificant speck of nothing?"

Claire remembers feeling a quick sweep of emptiness when Caleb said that. The flat sound of his voice, the way his words all ran together like the idea was too hard to explain. It was like he was saying something he never told anyone else. A kind of warning.

She wished she had told him stars never make her feel like that. Never. It's the exact opposite. Stars make her feel important. Significant. Like, *Here I am, right on this very spot looking up at gazillions of stars and I'm inside this gigantic universe and I'm me and I'm a part of all this.*

Maybe Caleb would've listened. Maybe he would've gotten this little smile in the corner of his mouth and said, *That's so you, Claire. You always think like that.*

And she could've said, *Sure I think like that. Because that's the way it really is.*

Maybe she could've convinced him to think that way too.

Everything could've been changed.

But just then Matt got to the top of the hill, his hat pulled down over his eyebrows, his long scarf coiled like a boa constrictor around his neck. "Come on, Claire! Last one down the hill buys coffees." He pulled her toward the edge and dropped his cardboard.

Even before they started back down the hill, Claire could see that Caleb had left.

There are still a few quiet voices at campsites around her. The guys from the van are sitting at a small fire, talking low, laughing. The girl must already be asleep. Claire is thinking about what it'd be like traveling with a bunch of friends like that. Everyone pretty much knowing everyone else. All the things that make them laugh or make them sad. She wonders if they argue much. For sure, it'd be way different than being with your sisters. Even though sisters don't know everything about you, they think they do. And how can you tell them everything anyway? They won't really get it in the exact way you mean it. With the exact way you feel.

Chapter Five

Hanna pokes her head into the tent. "You guys awake yet? I'm going for breakfast stuff."

Megan turns over and stretches. "Time's it?"

"Nine twenty. Claire? You awake?"

"No."

"Cute. You guys want anything?"

"A blueberry muffin and orange juice," says Claire.

"Get me a toasted bagel," says Megan. "Multi-grain. Cream cheese but no butter. And a small milk. Two percent."

"Be back soon."

"Leave the flap open. It's suffocating in here." Megan unzips her sleeping bag.

Claire is trying to come up with something to say because of last night. She knows how when Megan gets mad she can build a brick wall and stay behind it for days.

Hanna will notice and start asking what's up, and Claire will eventually have to admit what she said to her...and the way she said it. "I was thinking if Tajey didn't text you yet, maybe he doesn't have roaming. He's probably already in New York by now."

Megan sits up. "He didn't text me yet because he's not going to."

"You don't know for sure."

"I'm not delusional." She picks up a sandal and feels around the crumpled sleeping bags for the other one. "Anymore."

They're having breakfast at the picnic table when the girl from the van comes over. She's carrying a mug with a small tag from a tea bag dangling over the side. A couple of guys at her campsite are throwing a Frisbee and another one is between them, jumping and lurching to intercept it. There's a roar of laughter whenever he misses and tumbles. "I need a break from guys." She smiles and sits down. "I'm Mia."

"I'm Hanna. This is Megan and Claire."

"So you were the one who came up with the idea to dump the house-sitting job and drive across Canada," she says.

"We talked to Mia last night," says Claire. "In the washroom. When you were asleep." She glances sideways at Megan.

"I'd love to drive all the way to the Rockies," says Mia. She looks at Megan's sling. "What happened?"

"I fell."

When it's obvious there isn't going to be an explanation, Mia takes a sip of tea.

A loud cheer comes from the game, and they see a guy rolling on the grass, hugging the Frisbee. He stands up and takes an exaggerated bow.

"Alex," says Mia. "My whacked-out brother."

Another guy waves in their direction. "Hey, Mia! Ready to go? I'm hungry!" He tosses car keys into the air and catches them backhand.

"That's Jerry." She picks up her mug. "Well, see you later."

When she's far enough away, Claire says, "Alex is cute."

"Too immature," says Megan.

"Not the Tajey type?" says Hanna.

Megan ignores her. Tajey isn't up for discussion.

They get back to the campground at the end of the day and head for the swimming pool. Megan sits on the edge, far from the kids' end, and dangles her feet in the water. Hanna and Claire dive in.

When the camper van gets back, Mia comes over. "We met this girl who says there's a dance bar that's supposed to be pretty good. Rick all of a sudden thinks he's in love. Anyway, we're going tonight. How about you guys? Be great to have female backup."

Megan readjusts her sling.

"Hanna has ID, but we don't," says Claire.

"You wanna come, then?" she says to Hanna.

"I should stay here."

"You don't need to stay because of us," says Megan.

"Well, anyway, think about it. We're not leaving till about ten."

After they've eaten burgers and fries at a take-out, and after they've googled their route for the next day (Ottawa to Sault Ste. Marie), Hanna is still thinking about the dance bar. "If you're okay with it, maybe I'll go with those guys."

"I'm okay with it," says Claire. "Besides, we can just text if we need to."

"Ah...I don't actually have my phone anymore. I threw it away. When we were in Edmundston."

"Are you crazy?" says Megan. "Why'd you do that?"

"It's because of Mrs. Gallo, isn't it?" Claire looks over at Megan. "I know about Hanna getting fired and about the threats," she says to her. "I wasn't asleep when you guys were talking the other night."

"Things were getting even more nuts," says Hanna. "She obviously ignored the lawyer's letter."

"Okay. So you don't have a phone anymore. We won't need to text you anyway," says Megan. "Stop treating us like kids."

As the van leaves the campground, a few children are still running around in the dark, hiding and laughing and screaming.

Megan is texting with one thumb. Probably not to Tajey.

Claire has messages from Rachel and Cassie. None from Matt. "Think I'll go in the tent and read. Okay if I take the flashlight?"

When Megan comes in, all she says is, "Boy, am I tired." She settles into her sleeping bag and turns away from the light.

Around midnight, Claire turns off the flashlight and goes to sleep.

"You awake?" Megan is sitting up.

"Hmm?"

"Hanna's not back yet."

"So?"

"It's two thirty."

Soon they hear a vehicle on the dirt road. Headlight beams slide across their tent.

"That must be them," says Claire.

The tent flap is slowly unzipped and Hanna quietly crawls in.

"We're awake," says Megan.

"Ohmygawd, you scared me!"

"You smell like beer."

"That's because I was drinking beer, officer. I just came to get my pillow. I'm sleeping in Alex's tent. Good night, dear sisters." She crawls back out and zips up the flap.

"She's not actually going to sleep with that guy, is she?" says Megan.

Claire tries not to sound anxious. "It's her business. They're consenting adults."

"Don't you have to be sober to be a consenting adult?"

"You're exaggerating."

"You always defend Hanna, Claire."

Right. But this isn't just about defending Hanna. Claire doesn't want Megan's way of seeing things to sink in and take over everything. So tied up in rules and shock and disappointment. "I think I might be a bit jealous."

"Oh, like you'd have sex with that guy. What about Matt?"

Matt and I don't have sex. Not that she'd ever tell Megan that. Or anyone else. "I'm not awake anymore, Megan."

It's mid-morning before there's any activity around the van.

Hanna comes back, carrying her pillow and sandals. "Hey, you guys! We're going to a wedding in a bowling alley!"

Claire guesses the obvious. "Jerry's sister's wedding."

"Yeah! What a blast!" She puts the pillow on the table. "Mia says we can get party dresses at this secondhand place she knows for, like, ten dollars."

"We don't even know the people getting married." Megan says this like it's some kind of rule. If you do not know the people who are getting married, then you do not attend the wedding.

"Jerry says everyone'll be cool about us going. It'll be fun!"

"Right. Maybe it'll be so much fun you'll be the one who ends up in emergency this time."

"You are so tight-assed, Megan! You better take a good look at yourself and change things fast. Get a life. I mean it."

"At least I don't get drunk and sleep with guys I don't know. And I don't get blamed for having an affair with someone's husband."

Hanna drops her sandals on the grass and pushes her feet into them. "Look. I'm going to that wedding whether you guys go or not. Then after that, we can get in the car and drive right back home where everything'll be safe and normal and boring! Why did I even think for one second this trip could work? I should've left you guys at home!" She grabs her backpack and a towel, and heads for the showers.

"She's changed," says Megan. "Really changed. Ever since Italy. I'm glad we're going home. Maybe I can get my job back." She readjusts the sling at the back of her neck.

Claire watches Hanna walk toward the showers, each step hard on the dirt road. "I'm okay with going to the wedding," she says cautiously.

"Why are we even talking about this? We're supposed to be on this big-deal sisters road trip and now Hanna's suddenly best friends with all these people we don't even know!"

"We sort of know them."

"Listen to me," says Megan. "We. Do. Not. Know. These. People. They're strangers who just happened to be in the same campground. It doesn't make sense to go with strangers to some kind of ridiculous wedding."

"Why'd you have to be so mean to Hanna just now?"

"Oh, right. Blame this on me. Great." Megan gets up from the picnic table. "I'm going for a walk."

Claire's phone chimes. A text from Matt: *Mom said u called. I'll be ok. See u when u get back.* Meaning he's not okay right now and he won't be sending any more messages while she's away. She can feel a door closing.

Chapter Six

Alex is in the passenger seat, another thing to make Megan stew and fume even more. Hanna's guitar is in the van, so there's lots of room for Claire and Megan in the back.

Alex tries to get Hanna to make up a song about going to a wedding in a bowling alley, but she just laughs. He starts to sing in a voice that's more like a growl:

> Dig out your bowling shoes,
> Grab your favorite hat,
> Head down the highway,
> Tell ya where it's at.

"Come on. Give me some backup, here. *Tell ya where it's at.* Poom. Poom. *Tell ya where it's at.* Poom. Poom." He does a few exaggerated moves with his arms and shoulders.

"Okay, who's got the next verse? Claire, give it to us. Come on." He keeps moving and clapping. "Poom. Poom. Just start a line. I'll help. Poom. Poom."

She starts singing. *"Someone's getting married."*

"Great! You got it! Poom. Poom."

Her mind's blank. "I don't know what comes next."

"That's it! Perfect! Here we go:

> *Someone's getting married,*
> *Don't know what comes next,*
> *Maybe have a baby,*
> *Maybe...*

"Dead-end, Alex," says Hanna, laughing.

Megan is missing all this, or at least pretending to, looking out the window, plugged into her own music.

When they get to North Bay, it's almost dusk.

Jerry's uncle says they can stay at his place, with Rick and Steve sleeping in the van and Alex in his tent. "The girls," he says, meaning Hanna, Megan, and Claire, "can use the rec room." Mia and Jerry will stay at his parents' place, though they say they'll bail if wedding hysteria gets out of control.

The next morning, the girls head out to buy dresses at *One Night Stand*, the secondhand place Mia knows about. Megan keeps saying she won't go near clothes that had been on someone's sweaty body, but Mia eventually finds her a dress with the original price tag still attached. Perfect fit. Hanna's dress has a small rip on the side seam, so she gets a couple of dollars off. Claire can't picture herself in any of these dresses. Too much lace or glitter, or too many frills or bows. Barbie dresses. But Hanna pulls one off the rack and holds it up. "This is definitely you." When Claire tries it on, she can smell a hint of perfume.

After Jerry's sister and her man say, "I do," they throw the first bowling ball together to start the wedding tournament. Alex gets the prize for highest score while walking like a chicken. Mia, Rick, and Hanna's team place third and win temporary tattoos that they immediately stick on their faces.

Now, the lights are turned off over the bowling lanes and tables are pushed back to make room for dancing. Music blasts from gigantic speakers beside the stage.

The lining of her dress itches, and every time she moves, the thin straps flop off her shoulders. Claire pulls them up and tries to sit straighter. But she likes this dress a lot. The creamy pink color, the way the wide pleats sit flat against her hips. How it tucks in tight at her waist and scoops low at the neckline. She feels sexy.

"You're a not-bad bowler!" The kid has to yell to be heard. He sits down in a slouch and stretches his legs out as if he's taller than he actually is. He's wearing black jeans, a white T-shirt, and a gray linen blazer. His sneakers are bright orange. He looks about ten. "Your swing's a bit sloppy but your kickoff saved you!"

"I thought I forgot how to bowl!" yells Claire.

"What's to forget?" He looks down at his sneakers, crosses his feet at the ankles, then uncrosses them.

"You must bowl a lot!"

"LGBTQ Youth League! North Bay champs two years in a row!"

Claire lets that sink in.

He watches the dancers move through the rainbow glitter of the disco ball. The song ends and the DJ starts reading out special requests.

"That's your sisters with Jerry and those guys," he says in his normal voice.

"Yeah. Hanna and Megan. My name's Claire."

"I'm Stephan." He looks into his paper cup, then tilts his head back and drains it. "Want a drink?"

"Okay. Ginger ale, if they have any. Thanks."

When he returns with the drink, it isn't ginger ale.

"What's this?"

"A booze milkshake, basically."

"How'd you get this?"

"Subtle. Okay, I know I look like a kid, but I'm thirteen."

"Since when's thirteen legal drinking age?"

"Weddings don't count. Everyone drinks at weddings. Anyway, my brother's bartender. These are mostly milk."

Claire takes a sip. It tastes chocolaty, with a pungent sting at the back of her tongue.

The music blasts out again and they watch people dance.

Claire is thinking it's pretty amazing that Alex got Megan out there dancing with the rest of them. She isn't wearing the sling and she's holding her crowd-surfing arm against her waist. Alex is imitating her, joking around.

Megan stands out in the crowd, not because of her bandaged wrist and how she's protecting it, but because of all the usual things—her hair, her height, her confidence. Her body in that sleeveless and very short turquoise dress, tight over her bum. Watching her dance is like watching her swim. Weightless, silky motion.

Hanna's red dress is fun. The small ruffles on the shoulders and around the bottom flip and bounce as she dances.

"Want another one?" says Stephan.

"I still have some."

He comes back with two large paper cups.

"Come on," he says, when their cups are empty.

They squeeze into the crowd and start dancing. Claire watches the disco colors play against her arms and Stephan's face. It makes her think of soft rain. Hanna waves and she waves back. But a dizzy feeling begins to wash over her. The chaotic motion of people dancing. All those circling colors. She grabs Stephan's arm.

"Let's get outside," he says.

They sit on the steps of the bowling alley, and Claire starts to feel a bit more like herself. Not actually like herself. Not steady or solid or sensible. But at least nothing's wobbly when she looks up at lampposts or parked cars or people standing around smoking.

"I can't go back in there," she says.

"We could take a walk."

Not far from the bowling alley, they come to a red brick church. Stephan goes up the steps. "No one's here," he says. "They just leave it open."

Stained-glass windows illuminated by streetlights give the inside of the church a muted glow of blues and reds and gold.

"Think I better sit down," says Claire.

She closes her eyes. Except for the sound of Stephan quietly moving around the church, it's silent. A musky smell of wood polish mixes with the thick, sweet scent of lilies in vases near the pulpit.

What she remembers is that there was too much heat.

The church was packed with Caleb's relatives and neighbors, and just about everyone from school. Lots of people had to stand at the back.

Caleb's father spoke first. He said he wanted everyone to think of something Caleb did that made them laugh, because that's how he would want to be remembered. And then he said he was grateful for all the friends Caleb had. For all the fun they brought into his life.

Matt had something written down, but he left the paper on the seat when he walked to the front of the church. He stood next to Caleb's picture and the small polished box and the white roses. "All I want to say is Caleb was my best friend. He wouldn't do anything to make us all feel like this. Not on purpose."

She remembers that her eyes were closed. She could smell the dampness of melted snow on winter boots and heavy coats. She could feel the silent tension of everyone listening to Matt.

She leans forward and throws up into the lap of her creamy pink dress.

When Stephan gets back with Hanna and Megan, Claire is still sitting on a bench beside the church where he'd left her.

"This is all your fault, Hanna!" says Megan.

Hanna ignores her. Right now, she needs to get Claire back to Jerry's uncle's place. Clean her up and throw that dress in the garbage. "Can you stand up, Claire? That's it. Good." She brushes her hand softly over Claire's forehead. Then she wipes the mess off the dress and cleans her hands in the grass.

"What about where I threw up in the church?" Claire asks heavily.

"Perfect aim," says Stephan. "It all landed on your dress."

"Let's get a cab," says Hanna.

When they get to Jerry's uncle's place, Claire plunks down in a chair on the veranda. "I feel awful."

"Surprise," says Megan.

Hanna looks for the key in the planter where Jerry's uncle said it would be. "It's not here."

"Maybe he meant another planter."

"Another planet," mumbles Claire.

"Here it is."

That night, Hanna sleeps with her arm across Claire's waist so she'll wake up if Claire moves. In case she needs anything.

The car is packed and ready, and the three of them are sitting on lawn chairs in the backyard. There's no movement from Alex's tent. The van parked in front of the garage is just as quiet. Not far away, someone is mowing a lawn.

"You said we'd be going home after the stupid wedding."

"She didn't mean it," says Claire. "You were just mad, weren't you, Hanna?"

Hanna looks at Claire. How pale she is. What happened last night was so not her. Getting drunk, then having to wait all by herself like that in the dark beside that church till they got there. And what's this trip supposed to prove anyway? "I guess we should go back home. I'm sorry, Claire. You really wanted to do the whole trip."

"It's okay. I'm glad we at least got this far."

"Why do we have to wait till everyone else wakes up?" says Megan.

"It's called polite," says Hanna. "They're our friends."

"Friends. Oh yeah. Right. I forgot."

Claire takes a drink of water from a tall glass.

"Have lots of water," says Hanna. "It helps."

"Listen to the expert," says Megan in that tone she gets.

"What're you talking about?"

"Drinking. You're the big expert, aren't you? All those beers you had with those guys at the hostel. The whole next day you were hungover. Then you go and get drunk and have sex with Alex when you hardly know him." Megan is on a roll and keeps on going. "I bet you would've been drunk last night too, if Claire didn't beat you to it. She's always trying to be just like you anyway."

"Stop it, Megan! Just stop it!" For a split second, it looks like Claire is going to throw the glass of water at her. "You blame Hanna for everything! What happened last night happened to me! It had nothing to do with Hanna!"

"Hey, you guys, what's going on?" Alex is coming across the yard.

"No offense, but it's none of your business," says Megan.

"You all right, Claire? Stephan told us what happened."

"I'm okay. Sort of."

"Weddings are brutal."

"We're going back home," says Megan. "The car's packed."

He looks at Hanna. "Right now?"

"Soon."

"I gotta use the can. Then you and me'll take a walk." He heads into the house.

"You got a lot of stuff wrong, Megan," says Hanna. "I'm not a drunk. I don't have sex with guys I don't know. I'm not trying to be a bad influence on anyone."

Megan doesn't look at her. She fusses with the clips on

the bandage, thinking about wearing the sling till they get back to Halifax. Then, she'll make an appointment with Doctor Irwin and find out what she has to do before swim tryouts in September.

Alex comes back and puts his arm around Hanna. "Let's go."

The lawn mower is still humming from a few houses away.

A half hour later, they're driving through North Bay, following signs to the Trans-Canada. No one's saying anything. Claire pushes a pillow against the window and leans her head on it. Megan is listening to music on her iPod.

Hanna stops for gas and tops up the oil. She buys windshield washer and fills the container to the brim. She cleans the windshield and the rear window, then moves the car over to the air pump and checks the tires.

She stops at a drive-thru for coffee and bagels, and buys extra water for Claire.

At the intersection of the Trans-Canada, she signals left and turns. *West.*

"What're you doing?"

"Driving to Vancouver."

Claire quickly sits up.

PART TWO

Chapter One

Things are pretty quiet as they drive away from North Bay, Hanna and Claire cautious and Megan frustrated because of what Hanna called a "fair vote." One vote east. Two votes west.

That night they camp just past Sault Ste. Marie, then continue up and around Lake Superior, stopping late in the afternoon at Marathon.

"There's a campground not far from here. Neys," says Claire, checking the website. "N-E-Y-S." She scrolls through some reviews. "Listen to this. *If you have a sense of history, you will love camping at Neys, one of Canada's WW2 concentration camps.*"

"Great," says Megan. "Camping at a concentration camp. Everyone's dream."

"Check how far it is to Thunder Bay," says Hanna.

"It's...about three hours."

"We could keep going."

"It'll be dark before we get there," says Megan. "I hate putting the tent up in the dark."

"What do you care? You can't help anyway."

A dog is tied to the dumpster. A small beagle, sitting up expectantly, watching everyone cross in front of the alley. Beside the dog is a plastic bowl of water and a box of dog treats ripped open and mostly eaten. When Bear walks into the alley, the dog stands, wagging its tail.

He bends down and scratches its ears. "Waiting for someone, dog? Someone gone in the pub for a beer? Eh?" The dog leans into Bear's large fingers.

A note wrapped with string is on its collar. He unwraps the string and the note falls into his hands. *My name is Jake. I'm a good dog. Please adopt me.* The note is carefully printed in large, angled letters that, to Bear, look like a man's. Not someone his own age. And definitely not a child's.

He feels the water in the bowl. Warm. He dumps it and goes into the pub. "There's a dog tied to the dumpster out there. Can I get him some water?"

"Been there all day," says the guy behind the bar. He fills the bowl and passes it back.

Bear watches the dog lap up the water. He's a clean dog, brown and white with a black patch like a saddle across his back. His nylon collar is frayed, but the blue leash looks new.

"Need a walk?"

As soon as the leash is untied from the dumpster, the dog trots quickly out of the alley. He turns right and keeps on going. A couple of blocks away, he turns right again. They arrive at an apartment building, three storeys with bare patches of dried mud where a lawn is supposed to be. A couple of kids' bikes are tilted on their sides near the cement steps at the entrance. The dog starts up the steps.

"This home?" Bear slides his backpack off and sits down. He pats the dog's head.

It isn't long before two kids come out.

"Hey," says one of them. "Jake." Then he looks at Bear, immediately suspicious. "What're you doin' with Jake?"

"I found him. He brought me here."

"Mike moved out," says the other kid.

"This Mike's dog?"

"Yeah."

"Guess he doesn't want his dog no more." Bear stands up, puts on his backpack, and tugs on the leash. The dog resists. Bear kneels down, takes the dog's small face in his hands and looks into its dark eyes. "Mike's gone," he says. The dog licks drool off its mouth and glances nervously sideways. "Nothing here for you no more." He stands up and gives a firm tug on the leash. The dog trails along behind, looking back.

The kids jump on their bikes and start down the street after them. "Where you takin' Mike's dog?"

"Yeah!" shouts the other kid. "You can't steal Mike's dog!"

"I'm not stealin' Mike's dog."

"You're nuts!"

"For sure someone's nuts."

At the corner of the street, the kids stop following. Bear heads back to the pub and ties the dog to the dumpster. Then he goes inside and asks the bartender for a piece of paper and a pen. He scribbles his name and his auntie's phone number, then folds the paper twice. "If a guy called Mike comes in here looking for his dog, give him this, okay?"

The bartender tucks the note in a drawer without reading it.

"Not likely he'll come, though," says Bear.

When he gets outside, he puts the rest of the dog treats in his backpack and throws the empty box into the dumpster. "Here. Have another drink." Then he tosses the plastic bowl into the dumpster, too. "Let's go, Jake."

They leave the alley and cut across the street in front of the pub. The dog and the teen walk with the same posture, their heads down, their mouths solemn, their eyes focused on the space immediately in front of them. Anyone watching them make their way along the sidewalk, close to the curb and keeping their distance from others, would think they walk together like this every day. That they have long since learned the rhythm of each other's steps and know every turn and pause in the route they will take until they reach home.

"There's a campground right by the lake," says Claire. "Chippewa Park. We take Highway 61 and sort of go around Thunder Bay. It's got a beach and a wildlife park."

"You said we'd go to the place where Terry Fox had to stop running that marathon," says Megan.

"We'll still go."

"You have to reserve a campsite with a credit card," says Claire.

"Grab my wallet. Should be right behind my seat."

"How'll we see the monument? It'll be too dark."

"We'll go tomorrow."

"Booked!" says Claire. "Chippewa Park."

Bear stands at the end of the exit ramp, his arm outstretched, his thumb pointing west, the leash looped around his other hand. Jake sits next to him, watching traffic speed by. Every once in a while, the dog stands up as if expecting a car to stop.

When it begins to get dark, they turn around and start walking back down the exit ramp into Thunder Bay. "Don't get all guilty on me," says Bear. "Sometimes a dog means more rides. It's not your fault. People don't pick up hitchhikers when it's dark. Not Ojibway hitchhikers, anyway. Let's get some food."

Not that he has much money.

When Bear left home that morning, he asked his mother for thirty dollars and told her where he was going. His father and brother were fishing up on the river, so he didn't get to say anything to them about his plan. He'd be back in a month anyway, though his auntie might need him longer if nothing changes. If his uncle stays this way.

"I don't know how she'll manage," his mother said when she got off the phone.

"Auntie's the strong one," said Bear.

But then he got thinking about it. They were in that house alone, now, his auntie and uncle, with Uncle sitting in his chair and looking out the window, waiting for someone to knock on the door and tell them Lenny wouldn't be coming back home. "Suicide," Uncle had said the day Lenny joined the armed forces. "Suicide." Uncle's only brother had come back from Afghanistan in a coffin.

"Lenny and Edgar were set to paint the house this summer," said Bear's mother. "Where will Norma get money for hiring painters?"

So Bear decided to hitchhike to Pinawa and paint the house himself.

He left Lake Helen and got a ride down to the Trans-Canada. The couple that picked him up were only going to Ouimet and just wanted to ask about the canyons. If he'd known that, he wouldn't have taken the ride and end up stuck in the middle of nowhere. Bear is seventeen, but looks older. Stronger. Lots of drivers glanced his way and keep on going. It took hours before he finally got a ride all the way to Thunder Bay. The guy dropped him off downtown next to a pub.

When they turn off the Trans-Canada at Thunder Bay, streetlights are already on, though it's not quite dark. Claire is giving instructions for merging onto Highway 61, and Hanna is trying to pass a transport truck so she can get into the center lane. Megan is looking across the highway at a guy and a beagle walking down the exit ramp.

"*Terrance Stanley Fox*," says Megan, reading the inscription on the monument. "*Dreams are made if people only try.* I wrote a speech about Terry Fox in fifth grade and used that for my first sentence."

"Look at the sweat all down his face." Claire leans across the short fence that surrounds the monument and takes a low-angle shot.

"Think how far we drove," says Hanna. "He actually ran all that way."

"Farther," says Megan. "We didn't do PEI or Newfoundland or down past Toronto."

Claire snaps a close-up of Hanna and Megan. "Hey. This is actually a good one." She turns to a woman leaning against a motorcycle. "Would you take a picture of us in front of the monument, please?"

They stand, as they usually do for photos, in the same order, not even aware of it: Hanna, then Claire, then Megan.

They pass the exit for Thunder Bay and keep driving west. Megan is quiet. A different kind of quiet. Her earbuds are in her lap. In the rearview mirror, Hanna can see Claire texting. Maybe sending pictures to Matt, though she hasn't mentioned him in a while.

Megan unties the sling and slides it off. She removes the clips and unwinds the bandage.

"What're you doing?" asks Hanna.

"I don't need this. It's past a week."

"We should get your wrist checked first."

But Megan's arm is already bare. She balls up the bandage and clips inside the sling and hands it all back to Claire. "Put this in the garbage."

Claire catches Hanna's look in the rearview mirror. Instead of putting the bandage and sling in the bag with the apple cores and banana peelings, she tucks them under the guitar. "How's your wrist feel?"

"It's not sore."

Hanna pictures Megan in fifth grade, giving that speech about Terry Fox. Maybe now she's comparing herself to him and feeling foolish. "I'd say still take it easy," she says as a kind of comfort.

They drive a long time without saying anything.

Claire looks out at the forest, daydreaming about the stuffed toys people from school tied on trees near where Caleb died. Teddy bears and bunnies. Someone clipped five little red birds on branches. Christmas ornaments. Matt got mad because what did stuffed toys and bird ornaments have to do with Caleb? He wanted to take them all down, but Claire convinced him to just let it go. "I think it helps people feel better. Caleb wouldn't mind." By spring, some stuffed toys had been blown off by winter storms or were falling into soggy pieces. A small white bear, dangling from a ribbon tied to its arm, had become gray and matted. Those dark button eyes. A couple of red birds were still there on the branches.

She imagines Caleb standing in the rain beside the car when Matt was passed out at the lake. Not a ghost. More like a memory of Caleb. He wouldn't notice all that soggy and falling-apart stuff on the trees. He'd be too worried about Matt.

If only Caleb had said something to give them a chance to understand. Instead of being suddenly gone.

A pickup truck stops, and Bear opens the door. He puts his backpack behind the seat and climbs in, holding Jake. "Thanks for the ride."

"No problem. I got a beagle back home. Buffy. Hot day like this, she's flat out under a tree and a hundred rabbits wouldn't get her movin'."

"See," says Bear, scratching Jake's head. "What'd I tell you?"

"Say again?"

"Told Jake he'd get us a ride."

The driver grins and turns up the radio.

Jake sits calmly, looking forward. Every once in a while, he looks up at Bear, checking that things are still all right.

Last night, they slept on a beach near a campground, Jake finally settling down after the noise around campfires died out and there was just the easy sound of waves slipping onto the shore. Bear kept Jake's leash tied around his wrist as they slept. In the morning, before they headed back to the highway, they shared an egg sandwich Bear bought at a grocery store.

The truck is cruising along just above the speed limit when the engine suddenly revs. "What the—" The driver takes his foot off the gas, but the engine keeps revving. He pulls over and turns the truck off. "That was wild! Like the darn thing had a mind of its own!" He picks up his phone.

Bear opens the door and lifts Jake out. They walk along the shoulder of the highway until the dog stops and relieves himself on a guardrail post. Bear takes a bottle of water from his backpack, cups his hand, and pours water into his large palm. Jake takes a noisy drink.

"Looks like I'm stuck here for a bit," says the driver. "Could be I'll need to get towed. Might try your luck with another ride. I'll keep an eye out for you and your dog if I get back on the road."

Bear thanks him, grabs his backpack, tucks the water bottle inside, and starts walking with Jake following at the end of his leash.

Megan sees them walking away from the truck. "Stop, Hanna! Pull over."

Chapter Two

"That guy back there with the dog. I saw them last night."

Hanna eases the car to the shoulder of the highway. "So?"

"I think they're hitchhiking."

"You want us to give them a ride?"

"How far could he be going?" says Megan. "I mean, with a dog. It's too hot."

Hanna gets out of the car and shouts. "You and your dog need a ride?"

They're already running toward the car.

"Pop the trunk," says Claire, getting out.

"Going very far?" says Hanna.

"Pinawa."

"Where's that?"

"Manitoba."

"I don't think we'll get to Manitoba today."

"I can hitchhike from wherever you stop."

"Put your backpack in here," says Claire. She pushes with both hands against the tent and sleeping bags. "There."

When they're in the car, with the dog on the guy's lap, Hanna turns around. "I'm Hanna. This is Megan and this is Claire. We're sisters."

"Hi," he says. He doesn't smile and he barely makes eye contact.

"What's your name?" asks Hanna.

"Bear," he says.

Megan had turned around to look at him when he approached the car, but now she's looking straight ahead.

Claire tilts the guitar so it isn't like a wall dividing the backseat. The guy looks about nineteen. He's wearing jeans, a light blue T-shirt, and not-so-new sneakers. His thick black hair falls across his forehead. He holds the dog firmly with both hands. She considers reaching across to pat the dog, but decides not to. "What's your dog's name?"

"Jake." He only glances at her when he says this. His eyes a deep, deep brown. Calm.

Claire wonders if Megan will say something about seeing them near Thunder Bay last night. But maybe now that the guy and his dog are right here in the car, she feels kind of weird.

When they stop for gas, Bear gets out with Jake and walks over to an eighteen-wheeler idling beside the garage.

"What's he doing?" says Megan.

"Probably looking for a ride that'll get him all the way to Manitoba." Claire realizes she's hoping he won't get another ride.

"He's sure quiet."

"How come you wanted us to stop and pick them up?"

"I don't know. Just a feeling."

Bear and Jake get back in the car.

"Trying for another ride?" asks Claire.

"Thought he might be going to Manitoba."

"It's so hot," says Hanna, putting her credit card back in her wallet. "We should go somewhere for a swim."

"Why not find a campground and just stay there tonight?" says Megan. "It's almost three." She isn't actually regretting her impulse to pick up the guy and his dog, but it isn't like they'd be driving them all the way to Manitoba anyway. And it might be easier for them to get another ride while it's still afternoon.

"There's a provincial campground before Dryden," says Claire. "It's not far."

"You okay with hitchhiking from there?" asks Hanna.

"Sure."

They drop Bear and Jake at the side of the Trans-Canada near the turnoff. The heat and stillness at the edge of the highway are suffocating.

"Do you have enough water?" asks Claire.

"Yeah." Bear adjusts his backpack, wraps Jake's leash tightly around his hand, and starts walking.

"I can't wait to be swimming," says Megan as they drive toward the park. "Really swimming, with no sling." But she's thinking about Bear and Jake walking in that suffocating heat.

Claire is thinking about them too. Does he really have enough water?

Hanna stops the car. "I'm going back to get them. It's way too hot." She does a U-turn on the empty road and heads back to the Trans-Canada. "They can at least come to the lake for a while."

Bear and Jake are still near the turnoff.

Hanna leans on the horn until Bear turns around. "It's too hot for hitchhiking," she says. "Come to the lake for a swim."

He puts his backpack in the trunk and settles Jake on his lap. His smile is soft. Shy.

Claire is thinking about the contrast between Bear and the dog. How solid and tall Bear is compared to the very small beagle with the floppy brown ears. Hanna is thinking about living life like you mean it, not asking questions or expecting answers. Megan is wondering what made her look across the highway yesterday and notice a guy and his dog walking down the exit ramp like no one actually cared if they got where they needed to go.

They're close to Pinawa. Bear is second-guessing himself, wondering if this is a good idea, letting them drive him all the way to his auntie's place.

He thinks of the house. White's the worst color if a place needs painting. It turns a kind of gray and looks like something wild clawed at it, with paint scraped off the clapboard and around the windows. But he already told them he was going to paint his auntie's house, so they'd get why it was so scratched up and faded. There'll likely be more junk out by the garage than before Lenny left if Uncle's spending so much time sitting in his chair looking out the window.

He could've changed his mind when they got to the turnoff on the Trans-Canada. Said thanks for the drive and, no problem, he'd get a ride to Pinawa.

It's too late now.

Yesterday, at the lake, Bear didn't go swimming. He said he didn't bring his trunks but he actually doesn't know how to swim. Megan was a real swimmer. He couldn't stop watching her. The way she moved her arms. How she'd tilt her face sideways to take a breath. Perfect rhythm. Her feet hardly made a splash.

He rolled up his jeans and waded into the water, trying to coax Jake. The dog wouldn't budge.

It was Hanna who said he should hang out for the night. That he and Jake could sleep in the car and tomorrow they would drive them to the turnoff to Pinawa.

They went up to Dryden to get something to eat, and Bear bought Jake a couple of cans of dog food. Back at the campsite, they made a small fire. Hanna played guitar. It was low-key. Peaceful.

That morning, when they got in the car, Bear was wishing it was Megan in the backseat with him and Jake.

"Auntie's home," he says. "That's her car."

An old silver Toyota is parked in front of a garage that has a pile of junk by it. Nailed to the fence along the driveway, in carefully planned rows, are dozens of battered and faded licence plates: Friendly Manitoba.

The house is a small bungalow. Next to the front steps is a planter crowded with purple and yellow pansies. Thick woods, at the back of the house and on both sides, block out any sense of neighbors nearby.

"You can park in the driveway," says Bear.

Claire can guess what Megan's thinking. If she could see her face, it would have *Get me out of here* written all over it. Hanna's probably thinking this'll be interesting. Another road-trip adventure.

Bear looks over at the picture window. Uncle is not sitting there staring out.

They follow Bear down the driveway to the back of the house.

A stocky woman in white shorts and a red blouse rushes down the steps. "Give Auntie a Bear hug!" She holds her cigarette away from his back.

"Thought you'd be at work."

"Called in sick and that wasn't far from the truth. Sick with worry. Why don't you have a phone like everyone else? How can we know where you are? What if something happened? Call your mother right now." She turns from Bear, and smiles. "And who are your lovely friends?"

"This is Megan and this is Hanna and this is Claire."

"Sisters," she says.

"We're on a road trip from Halifax to Vancouver," says Hanna.

"Well. My, my. I suppose you look out for each other, though your mother would have a lot to say about giving rides to strange boys."

"Auntie—"

"How would they know who you are? You could be a criminal."

"We don't normally pick up hitchhikers," says Hanna. "This was different. Megan got us to stop because she saw them the night before."

"You saw us?"

"Yeah," says Megan. "At Thunder Bay. Looked like maybe your ride just dropped you off."

"So it was your idea to stop?" he says.

"I just got this feeling we had to."

Bear's auntie places her palm against his cheek. "That was Bear. Connecting. Letting you know." She starts up the back steps. "You must be hungry. I'll make sandwiches. Take the leash off that poor dog, Bear."

When the leash is off, Jake shakes his head and sends

a long shudder down his back. He trots into the house at Bear's heels.

The kitchen is small and tidy with a table and chairs in the middle and lace curtains at the window above the sink. A radio on top of the fridge is blaring. It's a call-in show and someone is saying, "...pay no attention whatsoever. They make their own rules."

"Your mom didn't say anything about a dog." She reaches to turn the radio down.

"I just found him."

"You girls good for tomato and bacon sandwiches?" She puts a frying pan on the stove and takes bacon out of the fridge. "Norma," she says. "I'm Norma."

"Where's Uncle?" asks Bear.

"Back working. Didn't miss so many days this time."

"May I use your washroom?" says Claire.

"Sure. Sure. You go ahead, dear. It's just there down the hall. Bear, put out a clean towel for the girls. And call your mom."

"Can I help?" says Hanna.

"You can make toast, dear."

"Hear from Lenny?" says Bear when he's back in the kitchen.

"He gets in touch when he can."

"How's he like the army?"

"Not so much. But it got him out of here."

"I'm gonna paint your house."

Norma stops poking at the strips of bacon and looks

at Bear. "So this is why you're here."

"Something to do."

She heaves a sigh and slowly turns the strips of bacon over. "Edgar won't be any help. He's got no energy. Don't know how he gets through his shift every day."

"I got all summer."

They take their sandwiches to the backyard, where there's a tilted picnic table. Norma leans down, puts a rock under one of the table legs and tests the stability. "There." Claire sits between Hanna and Norma. Megan and Bear sit across from them.

"You'll all need some of this," says Norma, holding up a small green spray bottle, "or you'll be eaten alive. The no-see-ums are murder." She sprays some liquid into her palm and rubs it over her face and neck.

Bear slides a piece of bacon out of his sandwich. "Here, Jake."

"What kinda name's that for a dog?"

"He had it when I found him."

"I think he looks like a Jake," says Claire. "Those floppy ears."

"He looks like *animosh*," says Norma with a laugh.

Bear smiles.

"Just making a little joke, dear," Norma says to Claire. "It means dog. *Animosh*. In Ojibway."

Dark clouds are crawling over the tops of trees. A crow caws from a high branch.

"That Lenny's crow?" asks Bear.

"Likely. Never goes far."

"Did you just say Lenny's crow?" Claire turns to see what Bear's looking at. A crow lifts off a branch and glides down toward them, then up again.

"It's Lenny's crow all right," says Norma. "Not afraid to come close." She tosses a corner of bread on the grass beneath the trees. The crow swoops and lands. It walks to the bread, picks it up, and flies back to the high branch.

Jake's eyes follow every movement, but he sits as if told to stay. Bear leans over and pats his head.

Hanna thinks about what Norma said: *It got him out of here.* "Lenny's your son?"

"See that window there at the end of the house? That's his room. The crow knows when he's home. Comes and pokes on the window. Wakes him up every morning. "

"I didn't know crows would do that," says Claire.

"Lenny was fourteen when he found that crow. Hunters were culling adults. No thought about any nesting babies. That one made it through. Lenny kept it in a cardboard box and fed it bread soaked in canned milk. Raw hamburger. First thing when Lenny calls home, he wants to know about that crow. Maybe that's all he calls for." Norma throws another piece of bread on the grass and the crow swoops to get it. "There's a bag of cookies by the fridge, Bear. How about you go in and get that for us."

As soon as they're in the house, Jake trots quickly into the living room. Bear follows when he hears a voice.

Uncle is sitting in his chair by the window. "So you got

here okay," he says. "This your dog?" He's holding Jake's head in both hands, ruffling his ears.

"Found him."

"Good huntin' dog."

"Where's your truck, Uncle?"

"Guy from work's got it. His car broke down so he drove me home and took the truck. You drivin' that Honda? Didn't know you got your licence."

"Hitchhiked. Some girls picked me up. We're out back."

"I'm good here."

"Auntie made sandwiches."

"No, no. I'm good."

Bear finds the cookies and goes out. "Uncle's home."

"I didn't hear his truck," says Norma.

"A guy from work's got it. Dropped Uncle off out front."

"We should maybe go," says Hanna. "Thank you very much for the sandwiches."

"They were great. I was really hungry," says Claire.

"Thank you," says Megan.

"You girl's aren't thinkin' of leaving? Look at those clouds. There'll be rain any minute. Lots of it."

"We'll be okay," says Hanna.

"Our first night on this trip we camped in pouring-down rain," says Claire. "We even went swimming. It was fun!"

Megan gives her a sideways look.

"You can't drive off with bad weather on the way. Not after bringing our Bear to us safe and sound. Bear'll sleep on the couch so you girls can have Lenny's room. Two of you'll have to sleep on the floor. You got sleeping bags?"

"We really do have to go," says Megan, giving Hanna a look that's close to panic.

But Norma won't budge. "Bring your things from the car." She picks up some plates and goes inside.

A sudden gust sweeps through the trees and a few raindrops fall heavily around them. There's a flash of lightning and thunder booms. Jake runs under the picnic table.

The drops of rain turn into a solid sheet.

Hanna, Megan, and Claire grab the rest of the dishes and run inside. Bear pulls Jake from under the table and runs in behind them.

Another loud clap of thunder shakes the house. The radio goes silent. The hum of the fridge stutters, then stops.

"Power's out," says Hanna.

Chapter Three

The rain on the roof is constant. From the window of Lenny's narrow room, Claire watches a jagged snake of lightning slither across the night sky. In the blue-white flash, she can see rain bounce and flip on the picnic table. Wind howls around the corner of the house, lifting and bending even the largest branches. She's soundlessly repeating, *Animosh, animosh.* Just moving her lips, trying out the way Norma said it. *Knee-mush. Knee-mush.*

Thunder rumbles far off.

Hanna and Megan are rolling out their sleeping bags. Two small candles Norma gave them flicker in jars on the bedside table.

"Soon as we wake up tomorrow, we're leaving," says Megan. She waves her hand over the candles. "Pine scented. Gross. Can I at least blow one of these out?"

"Stop complaining," says Hanna.

"Stop telling me what to do."

"Try having fun."

"Fun? As if."

Claire watches for the next streak of lightning. She's thinking of Bear. There's a lot she likes about him. How he rescued Jake. How he doesn't say much. The way he pushes his dark hair off his forehead and the way it flops right back. His height. His eyes. She knows he's mesmerized by Megan, but still she hopes they won't have to leave tomorrow morning. She glances at Hanna. Maybe she'll come up with some spur-of-the-moment idea that would actually keep them here longer.

Bear is talking with the sales guy at Pinawa Paint and Hardware. He already picked out the scrapers and paintbrushes. Hanna, Megan, and Claire are trying to find work gloves that won't make their hands sweaty.

It was Hanna's idea to stay and help Bear paint the house. "Just for a few days," she said as they were getting dressed that morning. "To help get him started."

"Why don't they hire painters?" said Megan.

"Do you notice nothing, Megan? These people don't have money to hire painters. And Bear's uncle's depressed about something. Norma said it's hard for him to even go to work. That's why Bear came all the way here to help them."

"I think we should stay too," said Claire. "I like Pinawa."

"You like Bear," said Hanna.

"I do not."

"Just sayin'."

"If we keep stopping, we'll never get to Vancouver," said Megan.

"Hmmm. Sounds like a song."

"Everything's a big joke to you."

"Everything's a big bore to you."

"Are we staying or not?" asked Claire.

"Let's vote," said Hanna.

When the truck turns into the driveway, they're working at the front of the house scraping off old paint. Bear and Hanna are on ladders. Megan and Claire are on the front steps, scraping around the doorframe and railing.

As he gets out of the truck, Bear's uncle looks confused.

The guy in the passenger seat gets out and walks across the grass toward them. His long legs are like stilts and his arms fall loosely as he walks. "Eddie, you've been keepin' secrets from me! Where'd you get your work crew? How ya doin', girls?"

Bear climbs down the ladder and walks toward the front steps.

"Eddie said he had a nephew here for a visit but he didn't say nothin' about girls." He holds out his hand to Bear. "Name's Lloyd."

Bear shakes his hand awkwardly.

"So you're from Lake Helen, are ya? The reserve. Norma's side of the family, eh?"

Bear nods.

"Well, Eddie," he says over his shoulder, "maybe I should stick around a while. Help take care of your workers here. Must be time for a beer. Hot day like this."

Hanna is watching from her ladder. She climbs down. "We decided to stay and help Bear paint your house," she says to Edgar. "Norma doesn't know we're still here either. We were asleep when she left for work."

"Come on," says Lloyd. "Let's get us some beers. How 'bout that, Eddie?"

"Think I'll have a rest. You take the truck on home and pick me up in the morning." He walks toward the back of the house, carrying his metal lunch pail.

"Ah, geez. Buncha party poopers. You girls wanna tour of Pinawa, give me a call. Eddie's got my number. Great trails up by the old dam. Big suspended bridge over the river. How long are ya here for anyway?"

"We're just helping paint the house," says Hanna.

"Okay, then." He walks to the truck. Long and lazy strides. "Can't be all work and no play!" he shouts back.

When he's gone, Bear climbs up the ladder.

Claire sees Edgar nodding off in his chair by the front window.

The next afternoon, Lloyd is with Edgar again. He gets out of the truck and goes around the side of the house to find them.

"Lookin' good," he says, standing at the bottom of Hanna's ladder. "The job, I mean." His laugh is like a cough.

Bear is on an extension ladder scraping the eaves.

"You girls got your tent pitched there in the yard, eh? Looks small. Any room to squeeze in one more?" He gives a gut laugh and a snort.

Hanna comes down the ladder and Lloyd is all eyes.

"So you girls are drivin' that Honda," he says. "They're good on gas, but I heard they're all over the road in a wind."

"It's okay so far." Hanna barely looks at him. "I'm going in for some water."

"I'll come too," says Megan.

Claire looks up at Bear. "You want some water?"

"Okay," he says.

Lloyd chuckles. "Think I scared them off."

Bear keeps working.

"Which one you got your eye on? How about the one with the curly, short hair? She's a cutie. Or maybe it's the one with the ponytail and those legs that don't quit." When Bear doesn't react, he says to himself, "Yeah, that's the one," Then he says, "Well anyway, guess I'll be goin'. Don't work too hard."

A few hours later, he's back again. Everyone's at the picnic table, finishing supper.

"Brought a two-four. A little thank you for the loan of your truck, Eddie." He clanks a case of beer down on the grass. "Who wants a cool one? Norma?"

"I'll share one with Edgar," she says. "You have supper?" She nods toward the barbecue. "Still some burgers left."

"Always room for a burger. And how about you girls? Want some beer?" Then he says, "Hey, I don't even know your names."

"These girls are Bear's friends," Norma says with a certain tone. "Claire. Hanna. And Megan. Girls, this gentleman is Lloyd, who works at the plant with Edgar."

"Well. Good," he says. He opens the case of beer and puts several bottles on the table, passing one to Norma.

"You go ahead," says Edgar. "None for me."

"Come on, Eddie," says Lloyd. "What's a half a beer anyway? These are on me. I'll get another case for you tomorrow."

No one else takes a beer.

"Looks like it's just you and me, Norma. Cheers." He tilts his bottle in her direction.

Bear goes over to the barbecue and gets a burger for Jake, handing it to him in small pieces.

Megan is watching Bear, but she's thinking of Tajey. His style. His confidence. How lean and strong he was. Bear is strong, too, but in a different way. He's quiet. It's like he doesn't even notice things about his own body. His height, his wide shoulders, his thick hands.

Hanna stands up as Lloyd reaches in front of her for ketchup. "I'll do the dishes," she says.

"Must be a machine can do that," says Lloyd. "You got a dishwasher, Norma?"

She holds up her hands. "God's dishwasher."

Edgar leans forward on his elbows. "So your car's fixed, is it?"

"Piece of junk," says Lloyd, his mouth half full of hamburger. He's watching the door close behind Hanna. "Sell me your truck, Eddie. I need a truck."

"Not for sale."

Lloyd finishes the burger and drinks the rest of his beer. "You start nights tomorrow?"

"Saturday."

"Hate workin' nights." Lloyd opens another beer.

"When you finish that, I'll drive you home," says Norma. "Edgar's tired."

"Lotsa time."

"I'm workin' tomorrow," she says.

He takes a small sip and looks around at everyone. Then he tilts his head back and drains the bottle. "I'll take this in the house for you." He picks up the case of beer and goes inside.

"That's a good job you're doin' there, Hanna." He puts the beer on the floor.

She doesn't turn around. "It's just dishes."

"And you're doin' a good job with your little sisters too. Takin' care of them."

"They're okay." She takes a slow, silent breath. "They don't need anyone to take care of them."

"Sure they do. Everyone does."

She knows he's moving toward her. There's a small sound, as if he's trying hard not to make any sound at all. She's waiting for something to happen. Instinctively. Her hands are still in the hot water, holding a mug and the dishcloth.

The pressure of his thumb is suddenly on the back of her neck. She almost laughs, like it's a joke. *Zap. You're frozen,* he might say. Then he'll laugh a sarcastic kind of put-down laugh.

She can't move.

His thumb begins to slide firmly, deliberately down her spine. Slowly, slowly down against the thin cotton of her tank top and roughly across her skin in the gap above her shorts until it stops at the top of her bum. He grabs the sides of her shorts in his fists and pulls her roughly against himself. His breath is in her hair. The stench of beer and cigarettes.

A piece of cutlery clangs on the back steps.

He moves away.

"More dishes!" says Claire, balancing a stack of plates as she opens the door.

Hanna quickly looks at Claire. Did she see what happened? But her expression is neutral. She goes out to pick up what dropped. "I'll dry," she says, coming back in.

"Better get outta here before I get roped into doin' dishes," says Lloyd with that cough-laugh. He goes outside.

Hanna holds the mug and dishcloth beneath the soapy water. It's like a slimy line is running down the middle of her back. She can still feel his body against her. She wants to take her hands out of the dishwater right this very minute and tell Claire exactly what happened. Say there's no way this creep's getting away with it.

But she doesn't move. She's silent. This feels too weird. Too embarrassing.

Too familiar.

Chapter Four

"**Y**ou see Lenny's crow, dear?" Norma and Claire are beside the sink, peeling potatoes. "I haven't seen him since you fellas got here. That's three days."

"I don't think I saw him."

Edgar's reading the newspaper at the kitchen table. He looks over at them.

"Usually he's around." Norma keeps glancing out the window into the trees.

At supper, Edgar asks Norma if she heard from Lenny.

"I'd tell you if I heard from him." After a moment, she says, "They're busy over there."

"Busy. Is that what you call it?" He gets up and leaves the kitchen.

Norma sighs and looks at Bear. "I'm telling you, I don't know how to bring Edgar up out of this slump." She starts clearing the table. "You hardly ate a thing," she says to Hanna. "After working hard all day."

"I'm not that hungry. It was really good, though. Thank you."

"Must be the heat," says Norma. "Takes the appetite right out of you."

Claire glances at Hanna. Maybe it is the heat making her so quiet. All day it seemed like she was just about to say something, then didn't.

"I thought with you coming here things would change," Norma says to Bear. "All of you working on our house. But now Edgar's got it twisted up in his mind if something happened to Lenny's crow, then…oh, I don't know."

"I'll look for Lenny's crow," says Bear.

"Me too," says Claire.

"There's crows everywhere. It'd be hard for you to tell which one's Lenny's. Though I could tell. He's got a little white spot over his eye. Just this one spot of white feathers. Oddest thing. But you have to be real close to see it. No one'd get that close without Lenny."

"If we take bread, we might get close," says Claire.

Bear and Claire walk through the tangled brush and into the forest at the back of the yard, looking up into the trees, throwing bits of bread here and there on the ground.

"Leave that," says Bear when Jake sniffs at the bread.

They stand very still, listening. A few small birds flutter and chirp close by. No crows. In the distance, a motorcycle gears up and speeds off. Kids are playing and shouting a few houses away. Claire closes her eyes and tries to hear the sound of Bear breathing.

He turns and heads back. "Come on, Jake."

"Are we just giving up?"

"We'll look some more tomorrow."

Hanna is washing the car and Norma is smoking on the back steps.

"No sign of him, eh?" says Norma.

"Where's Megan?" says Claire.

"In watching TV."

Bear and Jake go inside.

Claire begins to follow, but stops. She looks over at Norma, who gives her an odd little smile.

"Let's you and me help your big sister clean up that car. I'll get the vacuum." She takes a drag on her cigarette and stubs it out.

Megan hears Norma's car start and then leave the driveway. She quietly unzips her sleeping bag and crawls out of the tent. Edgar's truck is gone too. There's a haze over the sun. It'll be another hot day. In her pajamas and bare feet, she goes across the damp grass and into the house. No one is home now, except Bear. He'll hear her walk down the hall to the washroom.

When she gets back to the kitchen, he's there. He touches her arm with his fingertips.

She's been thinking about this. A fantasy, at first.

Daydreaming. Seeing herself standing this close to him. She can smell a sleepy muskiness in his T-shirt. She places her hand on his hip.

He watches her eyes, making sure. His lips touch softly on her cheeks, her nose. He's not breathing. He holds her face firmly in both hands and kisses her. She's surprised by the sudden pressure. The experienced weight of his mouth on hers.

On the way back to the tent, she's thinking that Claire will know. Not because it's Bear. She always knows when something's going on. If Hanna figures it out, she won't say anything, at least not right away, because of Claire. It's not like it has to be a big secret. How can she help it if Bear likes her and not Claire?

She reaches into the tent for her backpack. They're both still asleep. It's already too warm, so she leaves the tent flap open. Maybe this morning she'll just do a short run.

As they're setting up the ladders at the front of the house, a small boy on a bike comes into the driveway and skids to a stop. "My mom says to tell you there's a hurt crow behind our house."

Bear lays the ladder on the grass. "Keep Jake here."

Megan kneels down and puts her arms around the dog.

When Bear comes back, he's carrying a towel like a baby in his arms. He lifts a corner. It's Lenny's crow. Above one dark eye is a tiny line of white feathers.

"Auntie phoned around. Told people about Lenny's crow missing," he says.

Megan puts her hand against the towel. "How hurt is he?"

"Something's wrong with his wing. He's real weak."

They take turns checking on Lenny's crow in the cardboard box in the kitchen and trying to feed it bread soaked in canned milk. Most of the time, it sleeps with its beak tilted against the towel. Once, Claire thinks she hears a caw through the opened window, though it could've been a crow in the trees.

When Norma gets home and looks into the box, they realize they've been hoping too hard, not really seeing the situation for what it is. "Poor creature. Must've got banged up in that storm somehow," she says. "Don't know how it made it this long with coyotes and foxes around. And cats." The crow watches them though half-closed eyes, its beak gaping open. She lightly touches the feathers along its back. One leg jerks in a useless struggle. "I'm not gonna hurt you, sweetie. It's Norma. Remember?"

"What do we do, Auntie?"

"I'll call Lisa up at the clinic. See if she'll take a look at him."

The clinic is at Lac du Bonnet, about thirty minutes away. Hanna says she'll drive. Claire sits in front. Megan, Bear and Jake get in the backseat. Bear holds the box with the crow.

Even without an X-ray, the vet knows the crow's wing is shattered at the shoulder joint. "Acute dehydration has exacerbated the situation," she says. "I can only recommend that it be euthanized. I'm very sorry."

No one says anything as they drive back along the narrow highway. In the rearview mirror, Hanna sees Bear put his arm around Megan. Claire is checking her phone. She likely already figured out what's going on with Megan and Bear.

Claire has a text from Rachel: *Caleb's father started this blog. Check it out.* She clicks on the link.

My grandmother and my older brother both suffered from depression, not that anyone in the family called it that. No one could see it for what it was. No one asked. My grandmother spent half her life in her housecoat and slippers. When he was fourteen, my brother hung himself. I thought it would skip a generation. I was blind to any signs of Caleb's depression.

Signs of depression? Caleb? But he was a fun guy. Always clowning around. Always up for anything. Like the time he waltzed Ms. Veniot around math class, the chalk in her hand, her sensible shoes squeaking on the tile floor. She laughed, but she still wouldn't give him the three points he needed to pass the algebra test.

Claire reads the next sentence: *Many of the most overwhelming symptoms of depression are thoughts of worthlessness and hopelessness.* She pictures Caleb that night on Nixie's Hill and remembers what he said about the stars.

It's dark when they get back to Pinawa. Bear carries the cardboard box to the garage with Lenny's crow inside, still wrapped in the towel. They'll bury the crow in the woods behind the house tomorrow.

103

"It's a sign," says Edgar. "Something's happened to Lenny."

"That's just foolish talk and you know it," says Norma. "Suicide."

Claire turns quickly toward Edgar. Hanna sees the look on her face.

"He didn't listen to me. Nobody did," says Edgar. "I said it was suicide when he went in the army, and I was right. Suicide. Mark my words." He leaves the kitchen. They hear the bedroom door close solidly.

"We could call Lenny," says Bear. "So Uncle can talk to him and know he's okay."

"We are not calling Lenny. He'd think it was some kind of emergency."

"Or how about just message him?" says Megan. "Maybe he'd want to know about his crow."

"What good would it do to find out now instead of later? As if he doesn't have enough on his mind over there halfway around the world wearing a soldier's uniform every day."

In the morning, Megan, Bear, and Jake go looking for a rock. Something large enough to keep animals away from the buried crow. Something special to mark the grave. Claire is picking wildflowers at the edge of the woods. Hanna is on the back steps watching her and wondering if, because of what Edgar said last night, Claire dreamed about Caleb again.

They get back with the rock and Bear digs a hole at the edge of the woods. Claire places the flowers at the bottom of the hole to make a blanket against the dirt. Bear gently removes the towel and holds Lenny's crow in both hands. The body feels cool and stiff, the feathers soft, the bones fragile. He gets down on one knee and lays the crow on the wildflowers, then carefully puts soil back into the hole, handful by handful. The rock they found is dark gray, long and thick, with a patch of moss across one corner. When it's in place, it looks like a stepping-stone into the forest.

"I think Lenny will really appreciate what you've done," says Norma.

"We could send him a picture," says Megan.

"Thank you, dear, but I still think it's best to wait and let him know when he gets back home. He can stand right here and be near his crow in this place. The heat from the sun through those branches. Bird songs and the sound of their wings. Sweet earth smells. He'll be here soon enough." She is quiet for a moment. "It's too hot to think today. And I know for a fact it's too hot to be painting the house. Time for a day off." She lightly touches one of Megan's earrings, the small silver bird dangling inside the wooden hoop. "You're wearing those lovely earrings again. You had them on the day you got here."

In the afternoon, Bear asks if he and Megan can take Edgar's truck and go to the old dam.

"You've got no licence," says Norma. "And I know all about how you've been driving your father's truck on back roads since you could reach the gas peddle. But still..."

"I have my learner's licence," says Megan. She doesn't mention that she flunked the road test.

Norma heaves a sigh. "He won't like finding his truck gone when he wakes up. Make sure it's back in the driveway before he has to go to work."

"Thanks, Auntie!"

Not long after they leave, Hanna grabs her backpack and car keys. "I'm just heading out for a bit." She doesn't give Norma and Claire a chance to ask where she's going or why. She wants time alone. Since the other night in Norma's kitchen, she's been thinking about a lot of stuff she'd rather not think about.

She drives out of Pinawa and turns north to Lac du Bonnet. Yesterday, she saw a beach there with picnic tables and a long wharf.

She stops at a convenience store and buys a small bottle of orange juice, then goes to the liquor mart. She gets talking to the cashier, saying they brought Lenny's crow to the vet clinic and that it had to be euthanized and they buried it in the woods behind the house this morning. She knows she's talking way too much because of how self-conscious she feels buying three miniature bottles of vodka.

The cashier asks for ID.

In the beach parking lot, she drinks some orange juice, then adds the vodka to the bottle. She puts the miniature empties back in the paper bag and tucks it under her seat.

She goes down to the beach, kicks off her sandals, and

wades into the water, sipping from the juice bottle. A sweet wave of warmth starts to move through her.

She comes out of the water and sits in the sand. The juice bottle is more than half empty. She'll stay here for a couple of hours before she drives back. It'll be all right.

"Nice day for lazin' around. Left your little sisters back in Pinawa, did ya?"

Hanna instantly knows the voice.

Lloyd sits down, folding his long legs up in front of him, his hands on his knees. He's wearing a black T-shirt and jeans. Leather boots. Obviously not planning a beach day. "Drinkin' in public's not legal," he says.

She gives him a quick look that makes him laugh.

"Saw you at the liquor mart. Great meetin' place for drinkers." He grins. His eyes are large and round with dark bags like bruises beneath them. He hasn't shaved.

She looks out at the water. "Stop following me."

"Who's following anyone?" He leans back on his elbows and stretches his legs out. "Your car was at the liquor mart when I got there. Nova Scotia licence plates. Guess you would've seen me if you weren't so busy buying all those little bottles of booze and getting ID'd."

She grabs her sandals and gets up.

"Look, I guess you got your reasons for bein' so jumpy." He stands and brushes sand off his jeans. "I can be a real asshole when I'm drinkin'. But sober I'm mild as a kitten."

She dumps the rest of the vodka and orange into the sand, puts on her sandals, and walks away.

"Hope you're not thinkin' of drivin' that car. Someone might have to tell the cops."

She stops. With her back to him like this, she feels exactly like she did in Norma's kitchen. This time she will turn around. She'll scream at him never to touch her again. Each word will hit him so hard he'll be stunned. People will come over to see what's going on. They'll stand in a circle around her. They'll tell him to get the hell out of there. They'll stay until his car is out of sight and she tells them, *I'm okay, I can get home, that's my car over there, I'll be okay.*

But she doesn't turn around.

"Hey. I'm kidding about the cops. I wouldn't do that."

Kids are piling out of a van on the other side of the parking lot. A man herds them and their plastic toys toward the beach.

Her hand is trembling when she unlocks the car door. She drives away without looking in the rearview mirror. She's holding the steering wheel too tight. Her arms feel shaky. Her brain can barely catch up to each small move she has to make. Check the side mirror. Signal left. Look for pedestrians. Find signs to Pinawa.

Lloyd is sprawled on the sand beside her. He's smirking about the small bottles of booze. He's telling her he's like a kitten. He knows how afraid she is.

Dense forest darkens both sides of the road. There's no traffic. She pulls over on the shoulder and sobs into her hands.

Chapter Five

Claire is sitting on a chair in the bathroom wearing a plastic garbage bag like a cape while Norma swabs bright blue dye into a patch of her brown curls. The color is called After Midnight, which is why Claire picked it.

When she realized Hanna had left, Claire decided to clean out the tent. She hung the sleeping bags across the line to air out. She piled everything else on the picnic table—pillows, air mattresses, backpacks, odds and ends of clothes, a half-empty bottle of water, two red guitar picks, Megan's sneakers and sweats (still sweaty), the flashlight, and her book. She got a small broom from the house and swept the floor of the tent. She put everything back inside except the sleeping bags and her book. For a long time, she sat at the picnic table staring into the trees, her back against the edge of the table top, her legs stretched out, and the book open on her lap.

Though it was weird that Hanna had left by herself like that and it was depressing that Bear hardly acknowledged she was a person on this planet whenever Megan was around, Claire wasn't thinking about either of those things. She was thinking about what Edgar said last night.

He doesn't know anything about suicide. No one does. Not really. When it happens, it's like everyone's suddenly in this upside-down universe where nothing makes sense anymore. They try anything to take away the shock and sadness and confusion. Like hanging stuff in trees by the lake. That little white bear with the button eyes out there in rain and snow and dark nights, getting all gray and matted up. A little bear like that is supposed to be on someone's bed, dry and cozy and ready for good-night hugs.

Norma was reading and smoking on the back steps. She put down the magazine. "I got an idea," she said, and walked over to Claire. "There's nothing like having your hair dyed to boost a girl right out of a swampy mood." She took a long drag on her cigarette.

So they drove over to the pharmacy and spent too much time deciding which color to buy. Red? No. Too ordinary, even if was called Radical Red. Pink? Too harsh. Blonde? No way. There were rows and rows of blonde dye. Almond, Sun-kist, Honey Light, Honey Dark, Baby Blonde, Ash, Radiant Golden, Pure Blonde, Very Pure Blonde, Natural.

Natural? Claire wasn't sure this was such a good idea.

Claire saw After Midnight and suddenly she was keen to dye her hair blue.

On the drive back to the house, Norma held her cigarette out the window like she was signaling left. Every time she exhaled, she turned her head and blew the smoke out of the car. Smoking was the only thing about Norma that didn't fit. As far as Claire could see, she was always sensible and considerate and not one bit selfish. Like coming up with this hair-dying idea when she thought Claire's swampy mood was because of Bear and Megan.

Which it isn't.

"Maybe we should've dyed a patch on the other side." Norma is looking at Claire in the mirror over the bathroom sink. "To balance things up a bit."

"I like it this way."

Later, as they sit on the back steps, Norma keeps saying things like, "That blue's definitely your color, definitely." and "Wait'll your sisters see how trendy you are." She blows smoke into the air above their heads.

With the long afternoon behind them and the fun of dying her hair, Claire starts thinking she might tell Norma about Caleb. How he was suddenly gone and no one could believe it. She could explain that she almost hoped, because of Bear, because of the kind of person he is, rescuing Jake and hitchhiking all that way to paint the house and how much she's been thinking about him and wanting to be with him, that if he liked her as much as she likes him, then what Caleb did maybe would stop hurting and she wouldn't worry about Matt so much.

But Bear likes Megan, which isn't anybody's fault.

She wonders if Matt is maybe starting to feel better because of going to a counselor. If it had been an accident, it would be different. Shocking and sad and frightening, but not confusing. Because after an accident you wouldn't have to keep trying to figure out what made your friend decide to die. "It's not right that Edgar says being in the army is suicide."

"What made you think of that all of a sudden?"

"I dunno." She doesn't look at Norma. "I just did."

"His only brother died in Afghanistan. I don't think he'll ever get over it. War terrifies him." Norma lights another cigarette.

Claire pictures Edgar getting mad at his brother for joining the army and going to Afghanistan and coming home dead. He would've kept saying it was suicide. But it wasn't.

"Think I'll just go in and watch TV maybe." She gives a little yawn and a stretch so Norma won't see that she's suddenly determined to go in there and say something to Edgar that he probably won't like.

"Show Edgar your blue hair. Might cheer him up."

He's in his chair by the window. The TV's on but he's not watching it. "Your hair blue?"

"Norma dyed it."

"Oh."

She sits on the sofa and looks at TV. It's a ball game. "You like baseball?"

He just stares at the television like Claire isn't right there in the room beside him.

"I don't think you should keep saying being in the army is suicide." She knows he's listening because of the way he tilts his head up and looks out the window at clouds like he just noticed them for the first time in his life. "Norma told me your brother died in Afghanistan. I'm really sorry that happened and I know it hurt you and everyone in your family and all your brother's friends. But it wasn't suicide."

He looks down at his hands.

"If it's suicide, the person decides they want to die. It's not an accident." Her throat is dry. She swallows, but that doesn't help.

"You're too young to know anything about all this." He still isn't looking at her.

"My friend Caleb died in February. Wednesday, February 20th. It was a snowstorm, so school was canceled. He took his father's truck and drove to the lake, where they have a cabin. He put a hose on the end of the exhaust pipe and put the other end in through the window and started the truck and sat there and waited to die. It was suicide. He decided to die." She looks past Edgar to the clouds suspended against the bright sky. Her eyes start to sting with tears, but she won't cry. "When Lenny's crow died, it didn't mean something bad happened to Lenny. Soon he'll come back home, like Norma said. And every day you'll be able see him and talk to him and do things just like you always did."

Megan and Bear are on the wooded path not far from the suspension bridge. A family just walked past and the two kids stopped to pat Jake. Now their voices can barely be heard ahead of them. No one else is on the path.

Bear is holding Megan's hand. She's thinking about how rough and large his hand feels and how small her own seems inside it. He steps off the path and pulls her toward a tree. He leans back and she falls against him. He lifts her hand to his mouth and softly bites her knuckles. When she kisses him, a sigh comes from deep in his throat.

Someone gives two soft taps on the window and Hanna screams.

"Hold on there, honey. I'm nothing worth screaming at."

A woman is at the window. She's wearing a straw hat that shades a face carved with wrinkles. Her eyes are as clear as shallow water.

Hanna wipes her face with the back of her hand and opens the window the rest of the way. An orange car is parked on the side of the road in front of her.

"Are you all right? Are you lost?"

She knows she looks a mess. And this woman would've heard her crying. "I'm not lost," she says.

"Then that kind of crying has something to do with a man."

Hanna reaches back and grabs a tissue from the box behind her seat. She blows her nose, then takes another tissue and dries her eyes and cheeks. "I'm all right."

The woman is still bending down, her face just inches away. She smells of lavender. On her straw hat, a few fresh lavender sprigs are tied with a tiny bow. "Someone break your heart, honey?"

"No. It's okay. Really."

"Asking too many questions, am I? Yes, I guess I am." She straightens up and says, more to herself than to Hanna, "A habit I'm too fond of to quit any time soon."

They're both quiet for a moment. Hanna is starting to feel uncomfortable. Cornered.

The woman is thinking she can't just walk away and leave this young girl here by herself on the side of the road. "Any chance this whoever-it-is who made you so upset will be trying to find you right now?"

Hanna quickly looks back over her shoulder.

"Okay," says the woman, reading Hanna's panic. "What I can offer is for you to come along to my place and have a little break from whatever all this is about. I don't live far from here. And I'm not the wicked witch of the forest, I promise you that."

"Um...I..." Hanna just wants to get back to Pinawa.

"Follow along behind me. Before we come to the Old Pinawa Dam, we'll make a left onto a dirt road. A few bumps and we'll be at my place. Nice river view." She starts to walk toward her car, then turns around. "If you decide not to come along, I want to wish you all the best, honey. Take care of yourself."

The orange car pulls away and Hanna watches it go around the bend. She's tempted to just stay here for a while. Close her eyes long enough for the tension to start to drift away. But what if Lloyd takes this road back to Pinawa?

Chapter Six

A few miles along, she sees the orange car again. When she catches up to it, she doesn't pass. She decides that, when the woman turns off, she'll give a friendly little toot on the horn to say thanks.

But that's not what she does.

The orange car signals left, slows to a crawl, then pulls onto a narrow dirt road. Hanna follows until they get to a small cabin with a screened-in veranda facing the river.

"My name is Gwendolyn," says the woman when they're out of their cars.

"I'm Hanna."

"Pleased to meet you, Hanna." She lifts a couple of grocery bags out of the backseat. "Now, let's make some tea. Would you get the door for me, honey? It's not locked."

Gwendolyn makes tea with peppermint she pinches from

a plant spilling out of a wooden box on the veranda. "Here," she says, handing a few green leaves to Hanna. "Rub these between your fingers and inhale that wonderful fragrance. Pretty amazing, huh. After you've had this tea, you'll forget all about your tears." There's no judgment in her smile.

They sit in old wicker chairs. On a low table in front of them are two mugs, a teapot, a small wooden pipe, and a miniature plastic bag with a clump of dried leaves inside. Gwendolyn stuffs some leaves into the pipe and hands it to Hanna. "Don't worry, honey. There's no tobacco in this. I grew it myself." She winks and passes her a lighter.

Hanna lights the small pipe and slowly inhales. She coughs and most of the smoke is lost to the breeze. She passes the pipe back to Gwendolyn.

It's so quiet. The river slips by soundlessly. Though the sun is down behind the treetops, the air is still warm.

For a while they sit without speaking.

Hanna feels safe in this place. Gwendolyn is like someone she's known all her life. She has a strong urge to tell her what she's told no one else. "Back there when I was crying in the car, it was sort of about something that happened today, but not totally. It was partly about something from a couple of days ago and a couple of months ago. But mostly it's about something that happened last year. When I was at university. All of it's kind of scrambled together. I know that sounds crazy."

"This something that happened at university, I'm guessing you haven't told anyone about it."

"It was humiliating. I just couldn't."

"Want to give it a try?"

"So that's basically the whole story. I called Mom and Dad and they drove up from Halifax to get me. They didn't bring Megan and Claire with them. It wasn't exactly a family outing. I didn't tell them anything about what happened. I just said university was a waste of money. That I didn't know what I wanted to be anyway."

"You said CBC reporters came to interview the president of the university," says Gwendolyn. Wouldn't your parents have heard something about it on the news?"

"Dad asked me if the situation on campus—that's what he called it, *the situation on campus*—had anything to do with me quitting. I said I didn't want to go to a university where crap like that happens. By the end of October I got a job as an au pair and was on a plane to Italy. That didn't work out either."

"Not all men are pigs," says Gwendolyn.

When Hanna gets back in the car, the sky has lost all color except deep blue.

Chapter Seven

"**H**anna **does stuff** like this all the time," says Megan.

"No she doesn't. How can you say that?"

"What about when she stayed out all night at Peggy's Cove with her idiot friends, and Mom and Dad didn't know where she was?"

"That was grad night. They knew she'd be out all night. You always try to make every little thing Hanna does sound so awful."

"Okay now, girls," says Norma. "Your sister's an adult. She doesn't have a curfew. We can all go to bingo and she'll be back here before we get home."

"But Edgar's working," says Claire. "How'll she get in the house?" She doesn't like the feel of this. Leaving without knowing where Hanna is.

"The back door's always unlocked. No one ever bothers

anyone around here. We'll leave a note to say where we are."

"Come on, Jake." Bear puts the dog's collar and leash on. "We'll need a guard dog for the drive back home with all that bingo money."

"Won't be a joke if we win," says Norma, dropping a pack of cigarettes into her purse.

The light over the back door reaches across the yard to the picnic table where Hanna is playing her guitar. Not really playing. Strumming. She keeps starting over again. Humming. She sings part of a line, tries it in a different chord, then jots something in her notebook.

A car door slams and her heart lurches. Nothing in the driveway. Out front, maybe.

If it's Lloyd, he'll see it's just her car in the driveway. He knows about Edgar working nights and maybe he knows Norma always goes to bingo. He'll figure out she's here by herself.

She grabs her notebook and guitar and runs to the back door. She stops and listens.

A woman's voice, probably from across the street, shouts, "I'll call you tomorrow!" Another woman says, "Not before noon!" and laughs.

Hanna goes inside and locks the back door behind her. She puts her guitar and notebook on the kitchen table and goes to the living-room window. The street is quiet. She closes the curtains and checks to make sure the front door is locked. Her heart's still slamming in her chest.

It feels surreal being alone in this house, listening for cars, peering out through the curtains, hiding like any minute now some creep's about to show up. What does she think he'd do? Smash down the door? Crash through the house, yelling her name? Or maybe he'd stand out there on the back steps talking softly, his face close enough to the door to brush lightly against it. Saying what's she worried about all locked up in the house by herself when all she has to do is open the door to see he hasn't touched a drop of booze and he's mild as a kitten.

Cold shudders through her.

She needs to get out of here tomorrow. Somehow she'll come up with a reason that'll make sense to everybody.

When Norma's car pulls into the driveway, Hanna quickly unlocks the back door and casually steps outside. "Hey, guys, how was bingo?"

"We came this close to the big money," says Norma. "This close!"

Megan walks around the back of the car. "I can't believe you took off like that without saying anything."

"I just went for a drive."

"That's so typical. Like you're in your own precious little world and who cares—"

"Now, now," says Norma. "We're all here together, and everything's fine. Let's go inside. I'll make some tea."

"Thanks," says Claire, "but I'm gonna read in the tent for a while."

"I'll just get my stuff from the kitchen and stay out here too."

Megan rolls her eyes with exaggerated impatience and follows Bear and Jake into the house.

It isn't long before the tent flap opens and Megan crawls inside. "I am sooo mad. We have to leave tomorrow. I mean it."

"Megan?" It's Bear, and he's right outside the tent. "I'll explain."

"You don't understand."

"I had to show respect. It's Auntie's house."

"It's my body!"

Claire and Hanna look at each other. *What?*

"Please."

Megan crawls out of the tent.

Bear's voice is quiet, calm. Megan is trying to keep her voice down, but it's not working. From inside the tent, they can hear her side of the conversation.

"You should've asked me first."

A low murmur.

"It's my personal business."

A few words. Then a few more.

"You didn't even know what I'd say. And just in case you're interested, I would've said a big, fat no. N-O."

Silence.

"Look. I told you I didn't have a boyfriend, and it's true. Know why? Because I don't want a boyfriend. Not home. Not here. Not anywhere. I'm going to university in September and I'm trying out for the swim team. That's all I care about right now. I don't need any complications."

Another low murmur.

"All I'm saying is you should've asked me."

It's quiet for a while. Bear says a couple of words. He sounds sad.

Megan comes back into the tent, waits a few seconds, then looks out through the flap. "Good. He went in the house." She turns to Hanna and Claire. "What're you looking at me like that for? You heard everything. You know what's going on."

"We could only hear you. Not Bear," says Hanna.

Megan picks up her pillow and holds it on her lap. "Bear asked Norma if he could sleep with me in Lenny's room. Without saying one single word to me first!"

"And so you want to leave tomorrow," says Hanna.

"Wouldn't you? I mean, my god, I hardly know him and he goes asking his aunt if he can sleep with me. Asking her! Not me!"

Hanna turns to Claire. "You okay with leaving tomorrow?"

"Yeah. Sure. I'm okay with it."

"First one awake wakes us up, then."

The tent is lying on the grass and most of their stuff is packed and ready to put in the car when Norma comes out on the back steps in her housecoat and slippers. She lights a cigarette, walks over to the picnic table, and sits down. "Don't leave mad," she says to Megan.

"He should've asked me first."

"Bear was doing things the way he thought they should be done."

"And I'm supposed to be okay with that? Well, I'm definitely not okay with it! It's insulting!"

"We just think we should be going," says Hanna. "It's not because of—" She stops when Megan frowns in her direction.

"The boy's in love," says Norma. "Don't be too hard on him."

The back door opens and Jake runs across the yard. Bear stays on the steps.

"A few kind words would make an easier good-bye," says Norma.

Megan roots through her backpack as if she's forgotten something.

Norma pinches the end off her cigarette, steps on the ash, and puts the butt in her housecoat pocket. "Edgar will soon be home from his shift. I hope you girls'll stay and let him thank you for helping with the house. For stopping on your journey." She goes inside, touching Bear's arm as she walks by.

Claire puts the tent in the trunk. Hanna is leaning in to reach something under the driver's seat, but Claire doesn't see what it is.

Bear goes over and picks up an air mattress. He's

looking at Megan, but she's not looking at him.

"You guys got any more garbage?" Hanna has a paper bag balled up in her hands. "I'll just take this in the house then."

There's an odd look on Hanna's face. Claire thinks it's a hint that they should give Megan and Bear a chance to be alone, so she follows her inside. They hear Norma taking a shower.

"Do you think she'll say anything?" says Claire.

"Who?"

"Megan. To Bear."

"She's stubborn." Hanna puts the paper bag into the garbage container under the sink. "This is full," she says, though it really isn't. "I'll take it to the trash can in the garage." She lifts the garbage bag out and ties a knot at the top.

Claire glances out the window. She sees Bear take Megan's hand. Jake is beside them, looking up. "We have to stay in here for a little while," she says.

Hanna can see what Claire is hoping for—it's written all over her face. She's hoping Megan will say a few kind words to Bear to make an easier good-bye. And here she is, holding this garbage bag with tiny empty booze bottles hidden inside. It makes her feel ashamed.

"Check for exits to Winnipeg, Claire."

"What's to see in Winnipeg?" asks Megan.

"Portage and Main," says Claire.

"Which is?"

"An intersection."

Megan turns around to see if she's joking.

"We can get to Portage and Main from the Perimeter Highway. The 101," says Claire. "There's lots of exits off there."

Megan holds her arm out the window and lets the breeze run through her fingers.

From Portage and Main, they drive across the bridge to The Forks and decide to have lunch at a pub that has a patio. Some guys at a nearby table watch Megan walk past on her way back from the washroom. She has the red lipstick on now, and her hair is brushed out with one side tucked behind her ear.

"Didn't you have your Montreal earrings on this morning?" says Claire.

"No."

"I'm sure I saw you put them on."

Megan heaves a sigh and picks up a menu.

"She's only asking," says Hanna.

"I didn't know if maybe you lost them or something," says Claire.

"Look, I'm not wearing earrings. So what?"

"Now you're being defensive," says Hanna. "You're hiding something."

"If you have to know, I asked Bear to give those earrings to Norma. She said she liked them. End of story."

"That's so sweet," says Claire.

"They're only earrings."

As they drive out of Winnipeg, Hanna says, "Let's not take the Trans-Canada. Just to be different."

"Just to get lost," says Megan.

Claire zooms out on the map. "Highway 2 will be good. Go to Pembina just up aways. Go south on that to the 101, and then head west and look for signs for Highway 2."

On both sides of the narrow highway are yellow fields. A vast sea of yellow until it meets the blue prairie sky with foamy white clouds. A farm on the horizon looks like a kid's toy.

Megan has fallen asleep. A few strands of her hair lift up in the breeze coming through the top of the window. Her mouth is slightly open. Bright red lips. With her face relaxed like that, she doesn't look like a grouchy complainer at all.

In the mirror, Hanna sees Claire staring out at the fields, her chin on her knuckles. What's she thinking about? Maybe she's wishing things turned out different with Bear. No, probably not. She's too practical. But it'd be nice if something really good happened to her for a change.

The highway ahead is a straight line all the way to the horizon. No cars or trucks or tractors. No turns. No hills. Behind them is the same long, empty highway all the way back to where they've been. It gives Hanna an odd feeling, looking ahead and then looking back. Ahead and back. All of it the same, for as far as she can see.

She pulls over.

Megan wakes up and squints. "Where are we? What're you stopping for?"

"We're nowhere and I'm stopping for no reason," says Hanna. "Come on, you guys, let's get out of the car."

A black bird flies low across the road and lands on a stalk of yellow flowers at the edge of the field. It gives a long, shrill call. They can see its open beak and a brief trembling in its throat.

"Look how bright the red is on its wings," says Claire.

"Will someone tell me what we're doing?" says Megan.

"Listen." Hanna closes her eyes.

A breeze moves through the fields. The black bird makes another shrill call and flies away. There's a little *ping* sound from under the hood of the car.

"There's no one out here but us," says Hanna quietly.

"Gives me the creeps," says Megan.

"If we screamed our heads off," says Claire, "no one would hear us."

"Well, let's scream our heads off, then." Hanna takes a deep breath and lets out a scream that keeps going and going and going.

Megan covers her ears and squeezes her eyes shut.

Claire is so close to Hanna, the sound shudders through her. She starts to scream, too, her eyes wide open, watching Hanna. When they stop for a quick gulp of air, Megan joins in.

Their screams go out across the yellow fields and up into the heat around them. Hanna stops first, coughing and leaning over to catch her breath. For a moment, they all just look at each other, bewildered by what they've just done. Then, without a sound, Claire begins to cry, her face crumpled in pain.

Hanna puts her arms around her. "Oh, Claire, what is it? What's wrong?" Sobs move up through Claire's body and come out in a long, sorrowful wail. "It's okay. Shhh. It's okay."

Megan doesn't know what to do. She watches Hanna, listens to her soft words under Claire's loud sobs. She's never seen her sisters like this. Claire crying from so deep inside and Hanna trying to soothe her. It makes her feel helpless. Afraid.

Claire's tears fall against Hanna's neck and slide down.

The sobs begin to subside. She takes quick gulps of air, then a long, slow breath.

"Tell me what's wrong. It's okay."

"I…"

"What? Just say it, Claire."

"I'm scared."

"There's nothing to be scared of. We're here with you. It's okay." She reaches for Megan and pulls her toward them. "Come on. Group hug."

They stay together like that, squeezed close in Hanna's arms, until the only sound is the breeze moving through the grasses.

"I'm glad I'm here in the middle of nowhere with my sisters," says Hanna.

"Me too," says Claire.

"Don't say it, Megan."

"What? I wasn't going to say anything."

"Good," says Hanna. "Thanks."

PART THREE

Chapter One

"**You drive, Megan.** And you sit in front for a change, Claire."

"Me drive?"

Hanna's already opening the back door. "Yeah. Why not? This highway's just a basic straight line. And it's not like there'll be a traffic jam out here."

Claire is standing by the passenger door, shading her eyes against the afternoon sun, looking at the road ahead. Then she looks back down the highway. She thinks about Bear and Jake and Norma. Lenny's crow. Edgar's eyes when she told him about Caleb. Matt's message: *I'll be okay.*

Megan and Hanna are watching her. Waiting.

Claire turns and looks at them.

"I need a break from staring at the road." Hanna gets in the backseat and unzips her guitar case.

"Okay, then," says Megan. "I guess I'm driving. You're up front with me, Claire."

Megan sits in the driver's seat, thinking through everything she's supposed to do. Seat belt first. Start the car. Brake's not on. Shift out of park and down to drive. Hanna isn't watching her, but that doesn't mean she's not following everything she's doing. She signals even though it's a pretty ridiculous thing to do on this empty stretch of highway. Automatically she looks over her shoulder to check for traffic. The car leaps forward. She smoothes out the ride, and they're on their way again.

Hanna plays something soft and hesitant on her guitar.

Claire is quiet. Now, for the very first time, she really does understand that what Caleb did is final. Forever. Nothing feels real anymore. She's so tired, she can barely think.

Megan eventually relaxes about driving. The car's pointed west and there's nothing between them and the horizon except this highway with endless prairie fields on both sides.

Claire has fallen asleep, her head tilted against the window.

"Wonder what's going on with Claire." Megan is almost whispering.

Hanna remembers Claire's dream, and her promise not to tell Megan. She sets her guitar on the seat and leans forward, keeping her voice low. "I think it's about Caleb."

"People at school said he did it because his girlfriend

broke up with him. But that was way before Christmas. Or because he was flunking a bunch of courses and wouldn't graduate."

"Maybe it was something totally different from things like that. Whatever it was could be the reason he flunked those courses and why his girlfriend broke up with him."

"Like what? Drugs?"

"If he was doing drugs, people would know."

"Claire didn't say anything about him doing drugs."

"How'd she react when it happened?"

"All of us were home when Matt called. She was stacking the dishwasher. Dad was in the kitchen too. I was on my way upstairs and I heard Claire say, 'Oh no.' Then Dad said Mom's name in this strange way like something real bad happened. '*Marjorie?*' Like that. Claire just stood there holding her phone. She didn't cry. She didn't say anything. It was like she wasn't even there."

Claire moves her shoulder against the door and gives a small sigh.

Hanna sits back and catches Megan's attention in the rearview mirror. She puts her finger against her lips, a signal for them to be quiet, remembering that rainy night in Edmundston whispering with Megan about what happened in Italy, and Claire was awake the whole time.

Hanna looks out at the fields. Another farm is on the horizon, with neat rows of tall trees near the house and barns. Someone must've planted those trees for protection against storms. She's seen pictures of prairie snowstorms and dust storms, where you can't see anything except snow or dust. Blinding.

They come to an intersection with a stop sign and Megan stops, even though there's no traffic.

Claire wakes up. "How long was I asleep?"

"Maybe an hour," says Hanna.

"How about you drive now?" says Megan.

"You're doing a great job. Let's just keep going." Hanna passes a pillow to Claire. "Here. Tuck this under your head. It'll be more comfortable."

In Weyburn, Saskatchewan, they pitch their tent at a campground beside a river. Tomorrow, they'll reconnect with the Trans-Canada Highway at Regina and head for Alberta. If they leave early enough, they might make it all the way to Calgary.

"Maybe it's time to let Mom and Dad know we're on this trip," says Hanna.

Megan stops brushing her hair. "Mom'll have a fit."

"She might be glad. Us traveling together like this."

"In her car? Without her permission? And not minding the house like we're supposed to? I don't see glad in that picture."

"They have to know sometime."

"I say we wait and tell them when they're back home," says Megan. "We'll get there before them anyway, right?"

"Yeah. Right."

"What?"

"What do you mean *what*?"

"The way you said that. *Yeah. Right.* Like maybe we won't be back before them."

Now Claire is looking at Hanna too.

"I didn't mean that. I was just thinking we should let them know where we are. How about you text them, Claire?"

"What'll I say?"

"Just say where we are and everything's okay."

"You do it." She passes her phone to Hanna.

C, M, and me driving across Canada. Now in Weyburn, SK. House alarm on. Honda's great. Don't worry. All ok. xo Hanna.

The answer they get back stuns them: *We know about your trip. I'm following Claire on Instagram.*

"You must've approved her," says Megan.

"I did not. I know who I approve."

"Here's your answer," says Hanna, passing the phone back to Claire.

I follow as Morgan. Since February. In case. Your Dad and I love you all.

Claire pushes her phone into her pocket. "This makes me really mad."

"Mom just needed to know you were all right," says Hanna.

"She didn't have to be sneaky about it."

Hanna is thinking about Claire's tears and her deep, deep sadness. Instagram wouldn't have been much help letting their Mom know about that.

"Dad just texted," says Megan. "He wants a photo of us in front of some writer's house who was born here a long time ago. He sent the link."

"Let's do that now. After that we'll go get something to eat."

In the morning, as they drive north toward Regina, Hanna makes up a song about road signs, naming random signs—one way, dead end, ducks crossing, yield. Then she comes back to the chorus: *"But the only sign we need to find is Trans-Canada West!"*

Megan is in the passenger seat again. Even she tries a verse, working the words into some kind of rhythm: *"Stop, slow, do not pass, detour."* The song almost turns into a shout when they get to the chorus again: *"But the only sign we need to find is Trans-Canada West!"*

Claire doesn't join in, though she knows they're singing to help lift the weight of her mood. For seconds, she forgets to breathe. Then she takes a long, slow, quiet breath.

Maybe this is what Matt feels like right now.

Maybe this is how Caleb felt.

Chapter Two

Clouds, dusty blue and patched with white, lay across the horizon below a bright sky. "We won't get to see the Rockies," says Hanna. "At least not from out here."

Megan doesn't really care about clouds hiding the mountains. Nothing's going to make any difference in how Claire feels. Definitely not this thing Hanna's doing, trying to make a big deal about when they'll finally get to see the Rocky Mountains for the first time ever.

Claire's eyes are closed. Maybe she's asleep again.

Last night, she had curled up in her sleeping bag before it was even dark. Hanna had gone to a laundromat, saying they should stay at the campsite and take it easy. Meaning she wanted Claire to *take it easy* and Megan to stay with her so she wouldn't be alone. Cautious. Like holding a small bird's egg in the palm of your hand.

"What's making you so scared?" Megan kept her voice calm, like Hanna would if it was her asking. Just this once, she wanted to be the one to comfort Claire instead of Hanna.

"Don't you ever get scared?"

"I guess. Sometimes." She thought of dark streets, strange sounds in the night. Ghosts when she was a child. Megan didn't want to talk about how afraid she'd been when Claire was crying like that and Hanna was holding her and saying it was okay because they were there with her. How vulnerable she'd felt with all of them standing on the side of the road in a place they'd never been before and no one else around for as far as they could see.

"Nothing's ever happened to you to make you this scared."

The simple truth of this made Megan look away. It felt like Claire was now the older sister, knowing some overwhelming fact of life that Megan couldn't even begin to understand.

Claire closed her eyes. Maybe she fell asleep, or maybe she just wanted to be left alone to think about what she needed to think about.

"Wait a minute," says Hanna and starts to laugh. She pulls over on the shoulder of the highway. "Come on, you guys. We need a picture of this."

"Of what?" says Megan.

"You'll see."

Near the car is a Trans-Canada sign, the familiar number 1 on the white maple leaf and the arrow pointing west. "Come over by this sign." Hanna's grinning. "Pass me your phone, Claire."

Cars and trucks zoom by, blasting gusts of hot air.

"This is nuts," says Megan.

Hanna stretches her arm out as far as she can. "Smile!" She shades the phone from the sun so they can all see the picture. "Look at the horizon behind us. Really look." She waits. "They're not clouds. They just look like clouds."

"The Rockies?" says Megan.

"Right!"

"So?"

"We've been looking at the Rocky Mountains all this time and we didn't even know it."

Claire stares at the horizon, thinking about signs of depression right there in front of you even when you don't see them.

As they get closer to the mountains, Hanna keeps saying how gigantic they are. How the snow on the tops really does look like white clouds. How much fun it'll be when they're driving up into the mountains and down the other side.

Megan has totally given up on the exaggerated enthusiasm for the Rockies. Since yesterday, she's had this odd feeling of missing Claire, even though she's right there in the backseat. Hanna must feel like this too or she wouldn't be trying so hard to make things fun again.

They start to see road signs for Calgary, and traffic gets heavier. Hanna stays in the right-hand lane and closes her window against the noise of cars and trucks zooming by in the other lanes.

An eighteen-wheeler rattles past, then eases into the lane in front of them. Hanna adjusts the visor to block the sun. She slows down to widen the gap between them.

Megan and Hanna see it at the same time. Inexplicable. Bizarre. A metal object is gliding through the air toward them. For a split second, it looks suspended. Motionless. Hanna thinks she's looking at a boomerang. There's no time to lift her foot off the gas or touch the brakes. Suddenly, the object hits the pavement right in front of the car. In a shower of sparks, it skids and twirls beneath them.

Hanna and Megan don't speak. The eighteen-wheeler is still there in front of them. Traffic continues along as usual.

Finally Megan says, "What was that?"

"Something off that truck."

"I can't believe how it like all of a sudden just dropped and hit the road like that. Freaky."

Lucky, thinks Hanna. The piece of metal had hurled through the air toward them, not in slow motion like it seemed, but in multiplied speed, with the car going toward it as it was flying back at them. Until it dropped. Pure luck. It could've been different. She can picture each second as clearly as if it happened. A violent crash of metal through the windshield. Splintered glass cutting deep. The car out of control, careening off the highway, rolling over and over and over. In this imagined scenario, she doesn't hear their screams.

She glances back at Claire, who's sound asleep, totally unaware of how close they came to not being here at all. Megan's staring at the road ahead. Maybe she's picturing what could've happened too.

In Calgary, they find a hostel only a short walk from the city center. Hanna manages to get a family room with a double bed and a foldout cot. She knows Claire wouldn't be okay with staying in the room that has six bunks. Not right now.

Megan is putting on her sneakers as Claire wakes up.

Hanna comes into their room with a coffee. "Hey. You're awake. There's all kinds of breakfast stuff. Want anything?"

"Later maybe."

Megan checks her watch. "See you guys in about forty minutes."

Hanna takes a backpack off the chair beside the cot and sits down. "You feel any better?"

"I don't know."

"You should talk about this, Claire. It's not good keeping stuff inside."

"You keep stuff inside all the time."

"Like what?" But she's thinking about that creep Lloyd

touching her like he's doing her a favor. And what happened at university. Losing weight even before she left for Italy.

"Like what happened in Italy."

"I told you about that."

"Only because I heard you and Megan when you thought I was sleeping."

Hanna takes a sip of coffee and glances toward the window.

"I can tell there's other stuff you don't want me to know."

"It's not that. It's..." But, there *is* stuff she doesn't want Claire to know. Or anyone else.

The blue patch on Claire's hair is sticking up. Pillow hair. She looks like a little kid right now. How could she understand? Hanna considers going back to the kitchen for more coffee. End of conversation. She could at least tell Claire some of the stuff that happened in Italy. She knows most of it anyway.

"I started having dreams about Mr. Gallo," she says. "Stupid dreams that didn't make sense, but I'd see him the next day and get all red in the face. It felt like he knew." She stops. Not saying anything's way easier.

The first dream is still so vivid.

There was a party. People were out on the stone patio with the grapevine arbor and a view of the olive grove. Someone told her that Mr. Gallo was looking for her, so she went looking for him. When they finally found each other, he was standing at the top of the stairs and she walked up to him. He was wearing a white silk shirt with small blue flowers, something she never actually saw him wear in real life. He smiled at her. It was the way he smiled. He reached out and touched her face with his fingertips. When she woke up, she put her hand against the place where he had touched her in the dream.

"I don't get what's so confusing about having dreams."

"There was this...I don't know. Like this vibe. He'd be making coffee or doing something ordinary like that, and I'd start thinking about this dream I kept having and get all embarrassed."

"But how could that get you fired?"

"Maybe other people picked up on the vibe."

Hanna got the first text when she was in Milan for the weekend: *Stay away from my husband. You are girl garbage.*

Then more texts.

I know of the evil things you do.

And:

Dirt on the street is better than you.

And:

You are poison for my little girl. Never speak to her again. I will hurt you very much.

Hanna turned off her phone.

"There was this weekend I wasn't working, so I took a bus to Milan. I started getting these weird texts from Mrs.

Gallo saying keep away from her husband. Making all these threats. It totally creeped me out. Mr. Gallo was waiting for me when I got back. He said he was sorry, but I couldn't work for them anymore. I think he really felt bad."

"Didn't you tell him about the threats?"

"I tried, but he just wanted me to take the money and leave. It was like he was afraid she'd walk into the room any minute and find us there and think something was going on. He likely already knew about the threats anyway."

"That's so screwed up."

"I felt like it was all my fault. I know that sounds stupid. And for sure I didn't want anyone knowing I got fired. But Mrs. Gallo kept texting all this crazy stuff, so I showed it to Mom and Dad. I had no choice."

"You guys could've told me and Megan."

"I just wanted to forget about it."

"Doesn't work like that."

"Meaning?"

"Even if you try to forget, your brain just keeps remembering."

Hanna knows Claire is thinking about Caleb. "That's what happened yesterday, isn't it?" she says softly. "It was because of remembering Caleb."

Claire gives a small sigh. "It's like nothing's real. Everything's changed. I just can't trust things anymore."

Trust. Hanna's not expecting that. Claire maybe shouldn't even trust her. She walks over to the window and looks down into the street.

"Megan asked me about yesterday too." She gets out of bed and digs some clothes out of her backpack. "I know you guys are just trying to help, but..."

Hanna sees a police car pull up in front of the hostel. The back door opens and Megan gets out.

Chapter Three

"**Megan just got out** of a police car!" Hanna rushes out of the room and down the stairs.

"A police car?" Claire goes to the window. Megan is standing beside the car, talking to the officer in the passenger seat. Hanna joins the conversation. When the car pulls away from the curb, they all wave like they're old friends.

Claire is still by the window when Hanna and Megan come into the room. "Did you get lost?"

"She caught a thief," says Hanna.

"I didn't actually catch him." Megan sits down on the edge of the bed. "I was like just running on this street where there's no cars allowed, like this shopping street with restaurants, stuff like that. And there's this girl sitting on a bench playing a flute and she's got a straw hat by her for people to put money in. I'm almost up to where she is and this guy comes, like, outta nowhere and grabs the hat and runs. I'm running in the same direction so I just speed up and I'm next to the guy in seconds. I start yelling, 'Drop that hat! Drop that hat!'"

"That's hilarious!" says Hanna.

"Someone grabs him and that's when he drops the hat. Money goes everywhere. A security guy's there in seconds and calls the cops."

"So, how come you were in that police car?" says Claire.

"We had to go to the station and give a statement. After that they drove Charley—that's the flute player—to the Y. She's from Whitehorse. She just got here yesterday, like us. Anyway, then they drove me back here."

"Whitehorse," says Hanna. "Cool."

"She's busking to get money for a bus ticket the rest of the way to Toronto."

"Can we go see her play?" says Hanna.

"I know where she'll be this afternoon. For sure."

The bright notes of Charley's flute drift up and across the downtown pedestrian mall. She's sitting on a bench near a coffee house, her back straight, her legs crossed at the ankles, her hiking boots sticking out under her long, flowered skirt. In the straw hat beside her are a couple of dollars. One five-dollar bill. When she sees Megan, she manages a quick smile between notes.

They applaud when she finishes, and Hanna puts ten dollars in her hat.

"Hey! Thanks!"

"Charley, this is Hanna and this is Claire. My sisters."

"Hi, guys!" Her smile spreads across her face. Contagious. Then she notices Hanna's guitar. "You're a musician! Wanna play some tunes?"

"Sure. Okay." This is exactly what Hanna's been hoping for, though when Megan asked why she was bringing her guitar downtown, she just said, "You never know." She tunes her guitar. "You play something and I'll strum along."

"Hanna writes her own songs," says Claire.

"I don't really have anything worked up right now."

"Doesn't matter. Wing it."

Hanna looks at Claire and grins. She plays a few heavy notes, then starts singing. *"Dig out your bowling shoes. Grab your summer hat..."*

"She didn't write that stupid song," says Megan. "A guy we met in Ottawa made it up because he talked Hanna into going to this wedding in a bowling alley."

"The guy happens to have a name. Alex. And the three of us went to that wedding," says Hanna. "We got dresses at a secondhand store."

Claire looks cautiously at Hanna, hoping she isn't going to say anything else about that night.

"Do something you wrote," says Charley.

"Okay, but I don't have all the words for this. I'll just play it. It's in C minor."

Road Signs That Say West

The flute blends smoothly into the soft melancholy of Hanna's tune.

"That's so sad," says Charley when they finish. "Really. You can feel it."

"Yeah," says Hanna.

"You're an awesome guitar player."

"Thanks, but I need to practice more. A lot more."

"Everyone needs to practice more. Even the pros." Charley tucks her flute in its case. "You guys wanna grab a coffee? I could use a break."

An hour sitting around a small table in front of a coffee shop isn't much time to really get to know anyone, but Charley has a feeling she's picking up on who these sisters are. Or at least who they are right now. Especially Claire. She doesn't say much and she doesn't smile much, but Charley is pretty sure this isn't what she's usually like. When Megan and Claire go back into the coffee shop for refills, she says, "I get the feeling something major's bothering Claire."

"Something is." Hanna turns and looks past the red and gold Rosso Coffee Roasters letters painted on the window. She can see Claire standing behind Megan at the cash register.

"Sorry. Shouldn't snoop."

"It's okay. She...well, a friend of hers died in February. Suicide. Claire was doing okay, or we thought she was till a couple of days ago."

"That's what your song's about, isn't it?"

153

"I only wrote two verses so far. But, yeah, it's about that. I keep looking at her face when she's asleep and I think about all the stuff she's going through. Having dreams about. She's pretty confused. I wish there was something I could do."

"Finish that song and sing it for her." Charley has just enough time to explain her idea before Megan and Claire come back out.

"How about let's meet here around six and go eat?" says Charley. "After that, me and Hanna could do a few more tunes together. You guys in?"

Words for the last verse of her song are already starting to take shape in Hanna's mind.

A couple of people are standing in front of the coffee shop when they come back after dinner, and Charley goes over to talk to them. Megan and Claire sit at a table outside Rosso's. Hanna takes out her guitar and leaves the case beside them.

Charley gives Hanna a small notice printed by hand and photocopied on pale yellow paper. "This afternoon I put these all over the place," she says. "They made me copies at the Y. For free."

Did someone you know take their own life?
Did someone you know lose someone they love
because of suicide?
Come stand with us. 8 pm in front of Rosso's.

Hanna sees that Claire has picked up one of the notices, so she goes back to the table. "Charley made these." She lightly touches Claire's arm. "This afternoon I told her about Caleb. I...I was hoping you'd be okay with that."

Claire looks at the note again: ...*take their own life.* "I guess so. Sure."

"She's got this idea she thinks maybe could help...you know, help people feel better."

Charley stands on the bench and starts calling out for people to come and join them.

A few more people, some carrying the yellow notes, stop near the bench.

Hanna gets up beside Charley and reads the notice in a loud voice: "Did someone you know take their own life? Did someone you know lose someone they love because of suicide? Come stand with us."

Soon, a small group is standing in front of them.

A man in a suit and tie goes quickly past with his phone to his ear. Then he stops and turns around. He says something into the phone, puts it in his pocket, and walks over to the small group. A girl steps off her skateboard, tips it up, and holds it against her leg.

Claire and Megan stand behind the girl with the skateboard.

"Okay," says Charley. "Let's do your song."

The first notes are muffled by the street sounds around them. They play the intro again, a bit louder. Hanna starts singing.

Your face doesn't lie when you're asleep.
It tells me of the sadness that you keep
so deep inside
so deep inside.
I understand your sorrow when you weep.

A tragedy takes place when you're not there.
It fills you with confusion and fear
you try to hide
you try to hide.
I understand the sorrow that you bear.

Charley plays the break. Long, high notes. Hanna backs her up with guitar harmonies, humming softly. She nods for Charley to repeat the break. Then she sings the last verse.

Suicide is sudden. Reasons are unknown.
It leaves behind a grief that many own
for all their lives
for all their lives.
We're here so you will know you're not alone.
We're here so you will know you're not alone.

One single high note from Charley's flute lifts above the small group and floats up toward the pale reds and purples of the evening sky.

"A moment of silence," says a woman near the front of the group. "For all of us."

They stay quiet, though around them people keep walking, talking—some glancing at them over their shoulders, not stopping.

"That's a song I wrote for my sister," says Hanna, "because I want her to feel better. I don't want her to be scared." She turns toward Claire. Sees that she has taken Megan's hand.

Charley steps down from the bench. "Thank you, everyone. Thank you for standing with us. Take care."

"Wait! I have to say something!" It's the girl with the skateboard. She walks to the bench and faces the small group. "I have to say something." Everyone waits. "I'm not good at this." She takes a deep breath. "My friend Maggie's mother took a whole bunch of pills and got in the bathtub, but Maggie found her. Her stomach got pumped out so she didn't die. We were twelve. Maggie keeps having all these nightmares and the doctor wants her to take pills so she can sleep better, but she won't take them and that's four years of nightmares. I get real mad whenever I see Maggie's mother, but I don't say anything. Maggie doesn't say anything either. Anyway, I'm glad I came here on my way home. I could've gone another way."

Some people give an encouraging applause. Claire watches the girl's face, hoping it will tell her something, though she doesn't know what she wants to be told.

"I can't believe you wrote that song for me." Claire hugs Hanna and doesn't let go.

Megan's thinking about how Claire had taken her hand while Hanna was singing. The warmth of her palm. The feeling of being little kids and their mother always telling them to hold hands, Hanna then Claire then Megan, as they walked along together.

Chapter Four

"**A**lbertosaurus." Claire tilts her phone toward Megan. "They lived right here in Alberta 69 million years ago."

"Looks like T. rex."

"At the museum you can watch actual paleontologists cleaning dinosaur bones in this glassed-in lab."

Hanna is playing music with Charley at the pedestrian mall, promising to be back by noon so they can go to Drumheller. The trip to Drumheller is Claire's idea because of the dinosaur museum. Megan and Hanna have both picked up on this as a sign that Claire feels at least a bit better.

Which is exactly what she's hoping for.

It's easy to pretend to be obsessed with Albertosaurus. They've all seen *Jurassic Park 1, 2, 3,* and *4* and they'll likely see *Jurassic Park 20* if it ever comes out. Right now, Claire knows she needs to try to get back to normal, even if it's fake normal.

And she doesn't want Hanna to think her song didn't help because it did. The way she stood on that bench with her guitar and sang in the crowded street. Every verse real. *I understand your sorrow...* All those people standing together because they understood too.

She decides to text Matt. Waiting's just making things worse. She keeps it simple. Says they're in Calgary, that she posted some fun pictures of their trip, that she hopes things are going okay with him.

When she eventually gets back home, she'll try to explain what's been going on. How she keeps remembering things Caleb used to do like they're happening all over again. Her dream about when he died. And she'll tell Matt about Hanna's song and maybe about the girl with the skateboard.

"Charley got her bus ticket," says Hanna. "She leaves tonight. I asked her to come see the dinosaurs with us, but she wants to keep playing and get some extra money." She takes a cell phone out of her pocket. "Just bought this. Thought I should get reconnected."

"Good. Now you can text Mom and Dad," says Megan, "instead of it always being us."

"I texted them on Claire's phone."

"Once doesn't count."

"Let's drive Charley to the bus station tonight," says Claire.

"Good idea. I'll text her."

Still nothing from Matt. Claire knows she shouldn't be bugged, but she is. Even though he's going to a counselor and probably still feels pretty bad about everything, he could at least text her.

Maybe he's saying they don't matter anymore.

Maybe they don't.

Maybe they never did.

Matt was in eleventh grade, so he wasn't in any of her classes. She didn't really notice him until Beach Day, just before January exams, when he was goofing around with Caleb in the cafeteria. They were both wearing sunglasses, bathing suits, and flip-flops. Carrying pool noodles, blue and lime green, that they kept hitting people with. Caleb all of a sudden opened a cafeteria door and ran out into the snow. Matt didn't see him grab a fistful of snow, but he definitely felt it when it was shoved down the back of his bathing suit.

"What's so funny?" Hanna is looking at Claire in the rear-view mirror. They're waiting outside the hostel while Megan goes back in to find her sunglasses. "You've got this silly grin on your face."

Sylvia Gunnery

"It isn't really anything."

"Try me."

"I was just thinking about this time Caleb put snow down Matt's bathing suit in the cafeteria."

"Hold it. Snow? Bathing suit?"

"Beach Days."

"Oh, yeah. Forgot about Beach Days. Why do teachers think something lame like Beach Days'll take the torture out of exams?" Hanna's glad that Claire is remembering something funny Caleb did. Another good sign.

Megan gets in the car. "They're not there."

"You can get new ones," says Hanna.

"But they're my favorite sunglasses."

"Were." Hanna starts the car.

They cross the Bow River as they leave Calgary. The next time they cross the river, they're inside the mountain range, colossal rocky peaks reaching high into the blue sky, some still capped in snow.

"Three Sisters Parkway!" says Claire. "Did you see that? We have to stop."

Hanna quickly signals and takes the exit into Canmore.

"Go left." Claire gives directions through the town until they cross the Bow River again and drive along a road with mostly trees on each side and one or two small subdivisions. "Three sisters on the Three Sisters Parkway," says Claire.

"All this hype just because a road is called Three Sisters?" says Megan.

"It's not just a road, it's like it's our whole trip."

They stop in the parking lot of a mountain resort. "Let's get coffees here," says Hanna. "Bet they have a patio with a mountain view."

"Three Sisters," says Claire, scrolling through the Canmore website. "Big sister. Middle sister. Little Sister. See those mountains over there? Like in a row together? They're called the Th—"

"Don't say it again!"

"I think it's cool."

"Let's send a picture to Mom and Dad," says Hanna. "Stand over here so the sun's not in our eyes." She tilts her phone to get the three mountaintops.

"Maybe they sell sunglasses in this place," says Megan.

Hanna sends the picture with a quick message. They'll be surprised it's from her. And relieved.

At Banff, they ride the gondola to the observation deck at the top of Sulphur Mountain.

"Banff's like this miniature LEGO town," says Megan.

Claire looks down at the neat little streets. Rows of houses and patches of green. The bridge and the wide main street with shops and restaurants on both sides. Crowds of people, too far away for her to really see, are down there walking along the sidewalks, looking in shop windows, and talking about where to eat. She wonders how many of those people would listen to Hanna's song and understand.

A cloud moves quickly across the sun, its shadow rippling over the craggy peaks and valleys on the other side of the river. Hanna watches the shadow move farther and farther east along the mountaintops. Those mountains are like a huge wall separating her from everything that happened back there on the other side. Another reason she's right about the plans she made yesterday.

On the highway to Jasper, they see cars pulled over on both sides of the road. "Looks like an accident," says Hanna.

But it isn't an accident. Everyone has stopped to watch a huge grizzly bear. It's lumbering up a steep incline toward the forest, gazing lazily back as it moves along.

"Quick, get a video, Hanna!" says Claire. "You're closer."

The bear reaches the top of the slope and stops among low bushes, chewing at the tips of branches. After a while, it ambles into the forest and disappears.

Traffic starts to move again.

"Keep your eyes peeled," says Hanna. "When I booked our campsite, I saw this warning about animals in this park. Cougars. Wolves. Coyotes. That was a grizzly bear. There are black bears too."

"Better not be any bears where we're camping," says Megan.

"News flash—there are bear sightings all the time."

Their campsite near Jasper is at the edge of the woods, far from the registration desk.

"We can't camp here," says Megan. "Bears will come out of those woods and right into our tent."

"That's not gonna happen," says Hanna. "As long as we don't have food or anything to attract them, they won't come near us."

"As if bears know that rule."

"Unless you attract them here like you attracted a Bear in Pinawa."

"Good one," says Claire. She's already taking their camping gear out of the trunk.

"Look at my face," says Megan. "Am I laughing?"

Hanna opens the sleeping bags and spreads them on the picnic table to air out. She can feel the tension of the last couple of days starting to drift away. Claire seems like she's doing sort of okay now. Megan's still Megan, so that's normal. Maybe they can just chill and have a fun time for the rest of the trip.

Chapter Five

A **candle is burning** in the small glass jar on the picnic table, and a few logs in the fire pit warm the mountain night.

"Check this out, you guys," says Hanna. "White-water rafting. We should go."

Claire leans closer to see the pictures. "Looks fun."

"Fun? Like getting soaking wet and probably falling in the river and smashing your head on rocks is fun?" Megan hasn't even glanced at Hanna's phone.

"They say it's family friendly. Look at this. The kid in front looks about twelve."

"She's terrified."

"I'm booking for all of us. Just in case you decide to come and get soaked and fall in the water and smash your head on rocks."

The guide demonstrates how to walk up the small ramp to get from the pebbled shoreline into the raft. Everyone watches like it's rocket science. They all have on bright orange lifejackets and blue waterproof windbreakers.

"This'll be pretty exciting, hey," says Hanna to a little girl beside her. "I've never been white-water rafting before. Have you?"

"Nope. But my nana has lots and lots of times." She smiles up at the woman next to her. "Sometimes big waves splash right in the raft don't they, Nana?"

"Wow! Sounds fun!" Hanna looks at Megan, who's pretending she hasn't been listening.

One by one, they walk up the ramp and seat themselves around the sides of the raft. Hanna and Megan sit in front beside the little girl and her nana. Megan sits in the back.

The guide stands in the middle and steers the raft with very long oars toward the center of the river. "The Athabasca River originates right here in Jasper National Park at the Columbia Icefield," she says. "It's the longest river in Alberta. The water we're riding on right now eventually goes all the way to the Arctic Ocean. That's over 4,000 miles. But don't worry, we won't be going that far today." She grins when that line gets a few laughs.

They glide smoothly along, enjoying the peaceful wilderness with the forest of tall evergreens and spectacular mountains reaching into a clear blue sky.

"In fur-trading times, the Athabasca River and its tributaries were like a kind of Trans-Canada Highway. Hunters and traders and guides would've paddled through this canyon, probably looking up at those mountains just like we're doing."

The raft begins to gently nod and bob in the current. The guide pulls on one oar to keep them straight. A few small waves splash against the front of the raft and people joke with each other about still being dry.

Up ahead, the river narrows and curves around a rocky outcropping. Before they reach the bend, they hear the sounds of rushing water.

"White water," says Hanna.

Now, the guide has to work hard on both oars to steer them through the churning rapids. The first solid wave smacks against the bow and a heavy spray of water soaks everyone near the front of the raft. They all scream and laugh. Claire and Hanna turn to show Megan how wet they are when another wave leaps up and drenches them again. More screams and laughter.

"White-water rollercoaster!" Claire yells to Hanna.

Suddenly, the raft swerves sideways like a car skidding on ice. It keeps on turning until the front of the raft is at the back and the back is at the front. In one quick motion, the guide lets go of the oars, spins around to face forward, grabs the oars again, and continues steering as if nothing's happened.

Megan is staring at Claire and Hanna, frozen in shock. How'd she end up here? Another wave hits the raft and, for a split second, there's a lacy-white curtain of water suspended above everyone in the front. The curtain flutters madly, and collapses. This time, there are a lot more screams than laughter.

Another sideways skid and the raft spins again.

Back on shore, taking off their lifejackets and windbreakers, everyone's still laughing and talking about the rapids. The guide strolls through the group, getting videos of people's reactions. The little girl with her nana does a complete reenactment of the spinning raft and the sudden waves crashing over everyone.

Claire feels the back of her shorts. "My bum's totally soaked."

"Mine too," says Hanna.

Megan gives them one of her looks. "Like, we were just white-water rafting. Water. Get it?"

"Hold on. Stay right there." Hanna runs over to the tour bus and comes back with her phone. "We need a picture of our wet butts."

"I'll ask the guide to take it," says Claire.

The three of them hold hands and stand in a straight line, facing away from the guide. She turns the phone for a horizontal shot and zooms in. "Take a big bow, girls!"

Hanna's trying to write a song about their road trip, but it's just not working. The rhythm's jumbled and the words don't fit. She leans her guitar against the table and puts another log on the fire. Sparks fly up into the darkness.

"Our butts got more likes than anything I posted on this trip so far," says Claire. "Hey. Norma commented."

"Norma?" Megan looks up from her phone.

"I friended her a couple of days ago."

"Cool," says Hanna. "What'd she say?"

"Always thought you three girls looked alike."

"Too funny."

"You friended Norma?"

"She's my friend. I friended her. What's the problem? And check her photo. She's got your earrings on."

Megan only glances at the photo.

"They look really nice on her," says Hanna. "Think I'll connect with Norma too. And Alex and Mia."

"Don't forget Jackie and Adele," says Megan in her best sarcastic tone.

"You should message Bear," says Hanna.

"He doesn't have a phone."

"Send it to Norma. She'd be okay with that."

"Maybe I'm not okay with it."

"Wouldn't hurt to say hi," says Claire. "Here. Use my phone. Just say it's from you for Bear. If he writes back, I won't read it."

Megan finishes the message and gives Claire her phone. "I need my sweatshirt. Is the car locked?"

Hanna tosses the keys to her. "Get mine for me, will you? It's in the trunk."

"You writing another song?" says Claire.

"Sort of."

"What's it about?"

"Nothing so far." All she keeps coming up with are bits and pieces. Where they stayed. Who they met. How far they drove. Nothing that really matters. Maybe it's too soon to write about their trip. Maybe she feels too guilty.

"I like what it sounds like."

"What what sounds like?" Megan gives Hanna the keys and her sweatshirt.

"Hanna's new song."

"It's barely started."

Megan and Hanna are sitting at the picnic table with their backs against the top and Claire is cross-legged on her sleeping bag beside the small campfire. Two people walk by along the dirt road, the beam of their flashlight making a bright circle at their feet.

"This is my fave thing about this trip," says Claire. "Being by a campfire like this. Like it's our own little world." She tracks the path of a spark up out of the flames and into the night until it blinks out. "What's your fave thing, you guys?"

"Going back home and getting in shape for swim tryouts."

"Come on, Megan, you must have a fave thing. Like, so far, I mean."

"How about white-water rafting?" says Hanna. "Looked like you were totally thrilled out there on the rapids."

"More like totally tortured."

"I'm serious," says Claire.

"Okay. Let's be serious, then," says Hanna. She pictures

all of them dancing at Jerry's sister's wedding, but then thinks of Claire getting sick. "I'd say maybe..." Painting Norma and Edgar's house was fun, but now that she's thinking of Pinawa, there's that creep Lloyd walking across the lawn toward them. "Um..."

"See?" says Megan. "Even Hanna can't think of anything."

"Give me time." Then she has it. "I know. My fave thing so far was in Calgary when you gave me a big hug after I did my song."

"Aww," says Claire. "I love that you said that."

"And my next fave thing is Megan driving the car practically all the way from Winnipeg to Weyburn."

"I thought I did pretty good."

"Even Mom would've said you were excellent."

"Will you teach me to drive, Hanna?" says Claire. "I get my beginner's next month."

"Megan could teach you. She'll have her licence as soon as she takes the road test again."

"Why can't you do it?"

"Mom and Dad'll want you to do driving school like I did," says Megan. "It cuts way back on insurance."

"Makes sense," says Hanna. She finds a long stick and roots in the embers of the fire. "Should I put more logs on, or do you guys feel like going in the tent?"

"It's way early," says Claire. "Let's keep talking about our trip. Likes and dislikes so far."

"I definitely know one of Hanna's dislikes," says Megan. "Lloyd."

Hanna stops rooting in the fire.

"See? I'm right. Look at her face. He had the hots for you, didn't he, Hanna?"

"That guy was a total creep."

"But he did have the hots for you. Claire, you must've noticed that."

Hanna looks at Claire, then back to Megan. Part of her wants to tell them. Everything. What Lloyd did to her in Norma's kitchen. How he ended up on the beach beside her. The way he said *mild as a kitten*. She should tell them about the miniature booze bottles too. And about meeting Gwendolyn and smoking dope on her veranda. Then being alone back at the house and panicking because Lloyd might show up.

But all kinds of alarms are going off in her head, warning her to just play dumb about this.

"There's something I don't get. Not a like or dislike, and not about Lloyd." Megan shifts sideways to look directly at Hanna. "I don't get how you could sleep with Alex when you didn't really even know him."

"I didn't sleep with Alex. I slept in his tent. He slept in Rick's tent."

"You told us you were going to sleep with him."

"No I didn't."

"Why'd you stay over there, then?"

"Mia asked me to hang out by the fire with them, and Alex said I could have his tent so I wouldn't wake you guys up."

"But you did wake us up. When you got your pillow."

"Thought I could just sneak in and grab it without disturbing you guys."

"We weren't asleep when she came in the tent," says Claire. Maybe she can stop this argument before it really gets going and spoils all the fun. "You woke me up because Hanna wasn't back yet. Remember?"

"Thanks for worrying about me, Megan."

"Worrying? I wasn't worrying. I was mad! It was the middle of the night, for one thing. Plus, we had no clue where that dance bar was. And you didn't even have a phone!"

"Stop shouting," says Hanna. "You'll wake people up."

"I wasn't shouting."

Claire pulls the edge of her sleeping bag up over her knees and looks into the flames. "Matt and I don't have sex. We're just friend friends, not boyfriend girlfriend."

"What are you talking about?" says Megan.

The quick switch of topic throws Hanna off, too. "What made you say that?"

"I just felt like it."

"Why? Because of Hanna saying she didn't have sex with Alex?"

"Maybe." She gives another tug on the edge of her sleeping bag. "I guess I didn't want you guys thinking we were more than just friends."

"Were you and Caleb more than just friends, Claire?" Hanna can hear the caution in her own voice.

"Nothing was going on with me and Caleb sexwise,

if that's what you're thinking. I wasn't even like his close friend. But I could've been."

Could've. Hanna wishes she could see Claire's eyes in the darkness. They'd tell her a lot right now.

"This one night he talked to me about some stuff I'm pretty sure he never said to anyone else. I think he really trusted me."

"Stuff like what?" says Megan.

"A bunch of us were coasting over at Nixie's like maybe a week after January exams. For a while it was just him and me at the top of the hill. He was looking up at the stars, and then he said stars made him feel insignificant. That was his exact word. *Insignificant.* Just the way he said it, I could tell he was really serious."

"What did you say to him?" says Hanna.

"I didn't get to say anything because Matt came up the hill and wanted to race. Caleb left before we got back. He maybe thought I didn't get what he meant. Or I didn't care."

"He trusted you," says Hanna. "So he knew you cared."

"But he still did what he did." Her eyes fill up, and tears slide down her face. She can't stop them.

Only a few red embers are in the fire pit. The air is cooler, and no sounds drift out of the darkness around them.

Chapter Six

Something bumps against the picnic table. The candle jar falls over and rolls off without breaking. Megan opens her eyes. It's so dark it's like she hasn't opened them at all. "Hanna?"

"Stay very, very still." Hanna's voice is barely a whisper. "Don't make a sound."

Hanna doesn't have to tell her. She knows what it is. Her legs start to tremble uncontrollably.

Shuffling sounds move away from the picnic table and come toward the tent. A low *snuff snuff*.

Megan doesn't breathe. Tries to quiet the trembling. Her heart is pounding frantically.

How can Claire still be asleep?

Snuff. Snuff. Low along the ground. A small moan, like a question. It's right there on the other side of the tent.

Right there! Only thin fabric between them.

An eternity of silence.

Can she smell its rank breath?

It moves toward the front of the tent. Stops. Then pads slowly, slowly away. A twig cracks in the underbrush. Rustling sounds go farther and farther into the woods until they can't be heard anymore.

"It's gone," says Hanna, still whispering.

"It might come back."

"I think it'll just keep going." She doesn't say *until it finds food.*

"I can't stop shaking."

"Take a couple of deep breaths."

Megan gulps in air. "I was so scared."

"You were amazing, Megan. Really, really, really amazing."

"Hanna?"

"What?"

"Don't make this a joke."

"I promise."

"You guys won't believe this!" Claire has just come back from having a shower. She puts her towel and backpack on the picnic table. "A woman in the washroom said a bear ate a roast beef right out of their cooler last night! The whole thing! She said they heard everything from inside their tent. It scared them half to death!"

Hanna doesn't look at Megan.

"She said they had a huge rock on top of the cooler, and the bear just knocked it off and flipped the cooler over."

"As if a rock could stop a bear," says Hanna. "You're supposed to keep food in your car at night. It's right in the rules. Which they obviously didn't read."

"Just think, though," says Claire, looking back over her shoulder. "A bear. Somewhere right around here."

Megan pulls her sleeping bag and pillow out of the tent. "Let's get out of this place."

"That bear's likely a long way away by now," says Hanna. She sees the look on Megan's face. "But, yeah, I'm for packing up. Then we'll get breakfast in town."

"It's about five hours from here." They're on the Trans-Canada just outside Jasper, and Claire is doing a search for a campground near Kamloops. "They don't take reservations though."

"If they're full, there'll be other places," says Hanna. Not far from here, they'll drive out of Alberta and into British Columbia. Last province of their road trip. Three more days. The closer they get to the end of the trip, the more deceptive she feels. Not that she should've told them her plans before they left Halifax. Not that she's changing her mind. "Let's just take our time. We'll get there when we get there."

"Hey, there's a message from Bear." Claire passes the phone to Megan.

Hanna and Claire fake not being curious.

"He wants to know if we'll come back to Norma and Edgar's on our way home."

"It'd be fun to see them if we come back to Pinawa," says Claire. "And Jake and his floppy ears."

"I guess I'd be okay with it," says Megan.

"Two-vote majority," says Hanna, trying to smile. "Third vote won't count."

Claire sees the hesitation and she's sure Lloyd's the reason. "If you're thinking Lloyd will show up, we don't have to go back there."

"Should do something different, I guess." She doesn't know what else to say. For now, Lloyd will have to be her excuse.

"Okay, then. I'll just say we're not going home that way."

"Tell him thanks for asking, though," says Hanna.

"And say to pat Jake for me."

"You tell him yourself." She passes the phone back.

Claire writes a short note to Bear, thinks of asking about Edgar and Lenny and Lenny's crow or if he's going to bingo with Norma tonight. But she changes her mind. It's like none of these people seem real anymore. Like they're just in a movie she saw or in a book. All that's real right now is Hanna and Megan and this car and the Trans-Canada Highway curving and climbing up and down mountains, taking them the rest of the way to Vancouver. "Can we stop at Mount Robson?"

"Mount Robson? Really?" says Megan. "The same Mount Robson that's been like right there in front of us for the last couple of days?"

"There's a visitor center. And a hiking trail that has a really cool suspension bridge."

"I'm not hiking. There'll be bears."

"That seems a little paranoid," says Claire.

"Listen," says Megan. She turns around and looks directly at Claire. "You know the bear that woman in the washroom was talking about? Well, that exact same bear was right outside our tent last night. Wasn't it, Hanna? Like walking around and sniffing and sniffing. An actual wild bear! We could've all been mauled to death! So don't go saying I'm paranoid. You slept through the whole thing."

"It was on Megan's side of the tent for about three or four minutes," says Hanna. "She had to stay real quiet the whole time."

"I can't believe I didn't wake up."

"You always sleep through stuff," says Megan.

"We don't have to hike at Mount Robson," says Hanna. "We can just go to the visitor center and see what's there."

"Sorry I said that about being paranoid."

After Mount Robson, they leave the Yellowhead Highway and turn south. "Better get gas," says Claire. "There's this one town not far from here, and then there's like basically nothing after that until we get to Kamloops."

"May as well grab lunch too," says Hanna.

"We just ate," says Megan.

"That was hours ago."

As they head out of the small community of Tête Jaune Cache, Claire puts her phone on the seat beside her and looks out at the mountains. Back home is so far away. Rachel and Cassie. And Matt. She knows things'll be way different with him when she gets back. Maybe they won't even be friends anymore. Maybe, because they used to all hang out together, she makes him think of Caleb too much.

Chapter Seven

It's their last camping night, though only Hanna knows this. Claire and Megan know they're staying at a hostel in Vancouver for the next two nights. But they don't know what's happening after that.

The campfire is out and they've come into the tent. A wonky shadow of Hanna and her guitar is cast against the wall of the tent by the flashlight lying against her pillow. Megan is already in her sleeping bag.

"There's dolphins and seals and sea lions. And penguins from South Africa. Even a tropical rainforest." Claire is looking at the website for the Vancouver Aquarium.

"How about we do the aquarium Monday morning," says Hanna, "and then just hang out at a beach all afternoon?"

"An actual beach," says Megan. "That'll seem weird."

"There's one right in Stanley Park not far from the aquarium," says Claire. "Third Beach."

Hanna thinks about the three dimes tucked in her wallet behind her driver's licence. She had placed them there last October before going to Italy and that dead-end job. She'd believed she was leaving home for good, then— live in Italy for a year and who knew where she'd go next? When she noticed Claire's birthday year on a dime, she got the idea to find one for her own birthday and one for Megan's. A fun reminder. She may have even felt a bit wistful. Megan's dime, for some reason, had been the hardest to find. Hanna liked that the *Bluenose* was on the dimes too. Home.

Ever since they left Halifax, she's had this idea that they'd throw the dimes into the Pacific Ocean. Symbolic. Atlantic to Pacific. Maybe make a wish. They can do it at Third Beach. Perfect.

Then she'll have to tell them her plans.

For now, she'll just keep things positive.

"Hey, you guys," she says, maybe with too much enthusiasm. "Here's a question. Sort of like how Claire asked our fave thing about the trip."

"Talking about this trip's boring," says Megan.

"This is different. Listen." She lays her guitar down. "What's one major thing we hope for in the future? And not like making swim tryouts. I mean the future future."

"I don't have a clue," says Megan. "I can't think that far in the future."

"You're not even trying. What about you, Claire?"

"You go first."

"Okay then." Hanna doesn't need to stop and think. "What I hope for is I'll get to record my own songs. Not like be famous or anything. Just write songs and record them and sing in cool places."

"You could be famous," says Claire. "You're really good."

"I need to be way better. Especially with lyrics. And my voice doesn't have enough range. I should take singing lessons."

"Why don't you go back to university and take music?" says Megan. "Like Charley."

Hanna doesn't miss the dig about dropping out last year. "Charley wants to play in a symphony orchestra. That's way different than what I'm talking about. You don't need university to be a singer-songwriter."

"Right. Charley'll get an actual job and you'll be bumming around in no-name bars for the rest of your life."

Claire cuts off the argument before it bursts open. "In the future future, I hope I can be a counselor."

"You mean like at school?" says Megan.

"Not a guidance counselor. A therapist-type counselor."

"That'd be a depressing job."

"Not if you actually help people." Though it's Matt's personal business and maybe she shouldn't really tell them this, Claire wants to explain. "Right now Matt's going to a counselor because of Caleb. His mother told me when I called a while ago and he wasn't home. She said he got drunk and passed out by the lake and no one knew where he was till the police found him. Anyway, I've been thinking maybe the counselor's helping him. I don't know for sure because he stopped texting me. Like, totally stopped."

"He just needs some space," says Hanna. "When he gets his head around things, he'll start texting again."

"Like you did."

"A bit like that. Yeah." She gives a small sigh. But why go there again? "Okay, Megan. Your turn."

"It's not just hoping. I'm definitely going to be an athletic trainer and work with people who get sports injuries. Like at a clinic or sportsplex."

"I didn't know you needed university for that," says Claire.

"Four years. Kinesiology."

"Can you spell that?" says Hanna.

"K-I-N—"

"I was joking."

Claire's phone chimes. "Rachel," she says.

"Some professional teams even have their own athletic trainers," says Megan, "who, like, travel with them and everything."

"Thought you couldn't think that far in the future."

"Rachel's at this free outdoor concert. Look at these pictures. Amazing."

Hanna leans across her guitar to see. "That's not Halifax. Where is she?"

"Toronto. At her father's. Hey! Let's go there on the way home. Rachel's staying a couple of weeks. We could all go to a concert. Wouldn't it be cool?"

"I'm for that," says Megan. She unzips her sleeping bag and sits up. "They're just free concerts, so all we have to do is pick a band we want to see and get there for when they're playing. Simple."

"Gimme a sec. I'll check what's coming up." Claire is practically squirming with excitement.

"We'd be okay timewise, wouldn't we, Hanna?" says Megan. "I mean, we're in Vancouver for what? Two days? How long will it take us to get to Toronto?"

"I can't wait to tell Rachel."

Hanna can hardly believe it. After all this time on the road, with Megan griping about every little thing and Claire trying to hold it all together even while she was stressing about Caleb, finally they're both actually excited about the same thing. She can't just say they'll be in Toronto next week when they definitely won't. It's impossible.

"We're not driving back home."

Claire feels a sudden tight panic.

"What're you talking about?" says Megan.

"You and Claire are flying home and I'm driving to Whitehorse with a friend of Charley's. Her name's Kendra and she works there."

"You're kidding, right?" Megan looks over at Claire who

has stopped texting and is just staring at Hanna.

"No. I'm not kidding."

"So when's all this supposed to happen?"

"Tuesday. I already booked your flights."

"So," says Megan, "if it's Charley's friend, you must've planned all this in Calgary?" Then she knows. "Hold it. You wouldn't just suddenly decide to get us plane tickets back to Halifax so you could drive someone you never met to some place you never went to before, and then keep it a big secret. You knew you weren't coming back with us even before we left home, didn't you?"

"I thought a trip like this would be fun. Just the three of us. Drive and whatever happens happens." She doesn't say the rest: because eventually everything has to change and who knows if we'd ever do something like this again.

"But I don't get why you're not coming home." In the shadowy light, Claire's eyes look bruised.

"I need to see what's out there for me. Italy didn't work out, but that doesn't mean it won't work out somewhere else. I have to at least try."

"When were you planning on telling Mom and Dad?" says Megan. "Or are you dumping that job on us?"

"I don't want to mess up their trip."

"As if you care."

"I do care, Megan. You aren't paying attention."

"What about Mom's car?"

"I'll pay Mom for her car. Charley thinks I can get a job at the cafe where Kendra works."

"I don't believe this. You are so selfish, Hanna. You really are."

"She didn't have to bring us," says Claire. "She could've left us home."

"Why'm I not surprised you'd say that?" says Megan. "You never think Hanna does anything wrong."

"But..." Claire stops. She can see from the look on Hanna's face that this is pretty much what she thought would happen as soon as they found out. "I don't blame you for not telling us before we left. You knew it would change the whole trip."

"You got that right," says Megan. "For one thing, I wouldn't even be here."

Hanna's holding her hands in tight fists in her lap. She looks down and opens them as if letting something go. "I need to tell you guys something. So maybe you'll understand. It's about why I quit university."

Hanna opens the file on her computer: Psych 117 notes. The psych prof comes into the lecture hall, puts her coffee mug down beside the podium, and checks over her shoulder to see whether the screen is cooperating this morning. It is. *Human Behavior: Predict, Explain, Modify,* it says. With the highlighting tool, she draws a sloppy red circle around *Predict.*

A guy makes his way across the row of seats and sits beside Hanna, even though there are lots of empty seats in the lecture hall. "Oh, sorry," he says when he crashes against her desk. His smile is easy.

At the end of class, he says, "You catch the lecture Friday? I need some notes." He's looking at her screen.

Hanna's not keen to share the notes mostly because of the haphazard way she jots down words and phrases as soon as they drop out of the professor's mouth. She writes thoughts and questions that probably wouldn't make sense to anyone else. And they're her thoughts and questions anyway. Private. Personal.

"Ah..." is all she says.

"Like, could you just send me them?"

"Well..."

"What's your name?"

As she walks across campus, she decides that it's no big deal sending this guy her notes. They're just notes. If he can't figure out what everything means, that's his problem.

In the next psych class, he sits beside her again. She smiles. They've exchanged a couple of messages, so now he feels more like a friend than just another person in her psych class. Jarrod Graham.

When the class is over he says, "How about I buy you a coffee?"

There's nothing about Jarrod that would've made her notice him before he sat beside her the other day. No one in the class really talks much to anyone else. They just get there in time to be sitting like a bunch of keeners when the prof comes in, and they scatter as soon as class is over. But now that she knows Jarrod, she likes being with him.

Over the next three days, they go for coffee a couple of times, have lunch together in the cafeteria once, and take a long walk from the university almost to the other end of town and back. They study for the psych quiz in a small alcove of the library.

"How do you remember all those obscure statistics?" she says. "You must have a photographic brain."

"Just numbers," he says. He reaches over and gently touches the back of his hand against her cheek.

She almost moves out of reach, but stops herself, not really sure why she'd even react like that.

Jarrod lives off campus with another psych major, a guy he went to high school with. "Al's a slob," he says when he invites Hanna to the apartment, "so ignore the mess."

The apartment is in an old house that's divided into four units, all rented to university students. The couch on the veranda looks like it was dragged off the street from someone's garbage. They walk up the narrow stairs to the top floor.

"Al's home."

There's a lopsided plaque beside the door with two wooden circles on pegs below their names: Alan. Jarrod. Jarrod flips his wooden circle from OUT to IN. The circle beneath Alan's name is flipped to IN.

The door opens into a kitchen where a table by a window is piled with books, a laptop, an opened bag of chips, and a large milk container. Beyond the kitchen is a cramped space with a futon and a couple of beanbag chairs. A TV just about fills an entire wall. On the other side of this space is a short hallway.

"Hey. He did the dishes for once." Jarrod puts the milk in the fridge. "Washroom's at the end of the hall."

"I'm okay."

"Al's likely asleep. Skipping class again. Want anything? A beer?"

"No thanks."

Jarrod steps closer to her. "Can I ask you something?"

"Sure."

"Is it okay if I kiss you right now?"

Hanna smiles.

"You have to say yes or no."

"Yes."

His kiss is slow and gentle.

Al's bedroom door opens. "Oh. Sorry. Didn't hear you come in. Sorry." He walks to the bathroom at the end of the hall and closes the door behind him.

"The guy's timing's crap."

The toilet flushes and they both laugh.

Al goes back to his room. "Sorry," he says again, and shuts the door.

"Wanna order pizza and watch a movie?"

"Sure."

The next time Hanna comes to the apartment with Jarrod, Al's wooden circle beside the door is flipped to OUT.

Jarrod clicks on the TV, opens two beers, and sits beside Hanna on the futon. "Sitcoms are predictable crap," he says. "But the thing that's so smart about all that predictable crap is that the brainless masses suck it up like sponges. They don't even know it's crap."

"People just like an easy laugh," she says. "It doesn't mean they're brainless."

"Name me a sitcom that isn't brainless, then."

"Are we fighting?" She smiles and sips her beer.

"Fighting? Not me. Nope. Just having a conversation."

"Let's change the conversation."

"Let's forget about talking." He puts his beer on the coffee table, then takes her beer and puts it beside his. He leans and kisses her.

The door to the apartment opens and Al walks in. "Oh, geez. Sorry. Sorry."

Hanna and Jarrod both sit up.

"What'd I tell you about Al's timing?"

"I think you said it was crap."

"Ah, I could...ah...go somewhere."

"Forget it," says Jarrod. "Grab a beer, buddy. We're just watching this sitcom. Nothing serious." He laughs.

It's not long before Al goes into his room, making a lame excuse about needing sleep because of pulling an all-nighter last night.

"Where were we?" says Jarrod, leaning toward Hanna.

When he asks her if she'll sleep with him, she says no.

"I mean sleep sleep, like. Not sex sleep. Just cuddling.

With our clothes on." He puts on a dopey expression.

Hanna laughs. "Okay. Just cuddling."

His bedroom is very small. The twin-sized bed is squeezed in against a sloped wall under a dormer window. The only other furniture is a tall bureau painted black and a cluttered desk with a gooseneck lamp.

"Spoons," he says, lying on the bed. "You lie facing out the same as me. Curved the same way. Like spoons."

She lies down with her back against him. He puts one arm around her. "Looks like you've done this before," she says.

"Caught me." He nestles his face into her hair.

She's thinking there's no way this is going to be about cuddling. He'll move his hand along her arm to her belly. He'll wait for the least little signal that this could be about sex sleep and not sleep sleep. Maybe she should go back to residence right now. Avoid an embarrassing scene.

She hears soft, shallow snoring. She can hardly believe it. The guy's actually asleep.

At some point in the middle of the night, she wakes up, aware of Jarrod. He's kissing her neck and very softly saying her name. His palm is making gentle circles on her belly. A rush of heat washes through her. When he tugs at the zipper of her jeans, she turns toward him.

"You sure about this?" he asks.

"Yes."

Jarrod's not in psych class. The buzz starts through the room before the prof arrives. Everyone's checking Jarrod's Facebook page. A few people are laughing. Hanna hears someone say, "I don't believe this guy." She opens his page and starts reading.

A Field Experiment in Two Parts,
by Jarrod Graham, Psychology 117
Part 1: Freshmen Dating and Sexual Intercourse
Part 2: Facebook Response to Part 1 Report

Part 1 Report

Hypothesis: Females new to campus life are more likely to consent than not to consent to sexual intercourse within a ten-day period in which they have participated willingly in casual and non-sexual dating activities. *

* For the purposes of this study, "dating activities" or "dates" are real-time events (not digital/ electronic connections), such as: going for coffee, walks, cafeteria lunches, watching a movie at my apartment, or study dates.

Parameters of Part 1 of this research:
• Number of research participants: 6
• Duration of research: 30 days

- Age variable: 17–18
- Sexual experience variable: (information not reliable/measureable except to note that one female did not have previous sexual intercourse experience; this virgin variable did not correlate in any significant way with other variables)
- There were no independent variables

Basic findings from Part 1 of this research:
- Minimum number of dates before sexual intercourse: 2
- Maximum number of dates before sexual intercourse: 7
- Number of females not having sexual intercourse during study: 2
- Note: to protect the identity of all participants, I use only the first initial of either the participant's first name or last name. The participants, in order of study, are: N, E, S, J, A, and H.

H. *Hanna.*
She has a sudden urge to throw up.

Part 2 Hypothesis: To avoid influencing/contaminating the results of Part 2 of this field experiment, I am not posting my hypothesis about Facebook response to Part 1. All comments and questions are welcome.

The comments are predictable. Girls are calling Jarrod a jerk and guys are making crude jokes. There are some variations. Girls who say the four females who had sex with Jarrod are naive/stupid/gullible and guys who say Jarrod should be charged with harassment/stalking/assault.

Then it gets worse.

Someone says Jarrod can't prove anything. How do they know he isn't just making all this up? He has an answer. *The guy I share the apartment with agreed to always be home when sex was part of the plan. It's a small apartment. There are no secrets.*

Then it gets even worse.

Comments start on Twitter. *#psychedout.* Someone tweets that it'd be easy to track down the girls who "dated" Jarrod in the last thirty days. That maybe it could be like a contest to see how long it takes for photos of the six girls to get posted. That even though they'll all say they didn't have sex with him, it wouldn't take much to find out who's lying.

Psych class is about half over when someone posts Samantha Mason's picture: *I'm guessing this is S.*

A few minutes later, a girl gets up and rushes out of the lecture theater. Samantha.

Hanna can't think straight. Her face is red hot and there's a tight knot in her gut. She keeps her head down and her eyes on her computer. *Please, please, please, don't let anyone guess H.*

The prof's lecture is just a droning sound in the

background. No one's paying attention anymore.

Twenty minutes left in the class.

Hanna can't just get up and leave. That would be a complete giveaway. She keeps her head down, staring at her computer, pretending to take notes. Her long hair falls across her cheeks, a curtain to hide behind.

A photo is posted of a girl with long brown hair, but someone immediately comments: *Nadia's my best friend. For sure she's not N.* Then someone else comments: *I think I saw him with a girl who looks a bit like Nadia though.*

They're so close. The knots in Hanna's stomach get tighter.

"Read chapters 7 to 9 for next class," says the prof, finally, "and bring me one insightful statement about something you've learned from those pages. Original. Not plagiarized." Even before she's packed up her notes and picked up her coffee mug, most of the class is already outside the lecture hall.

Hanna hasn't moved. She's trying to figure out how to get from this chair, out of the lecture hall, down the stairs, and all the way across campus to her dorm room without seeing or speaking to anyone. If she's the last to leave, that'll be way too conspicuous. She takes a deep breath, stands up, and walks out of the lecture hall.

A few people are standing right outside the door beside a window, all looking at their phones. One guy laughs. She hears a girl say, "This is not one bit funny, you guys." The girl leaves the group and starts walking down the hall.

Hanna walks slowly behind her, still trying not to be conspicuous, but now feeling a small sense of comfort. This girl, whoever she is, is on her side.

The whole way across campus, she doesn't look at her phone. As she turns the key to her dorm room, the door opposite opens and Becky steps cautiously out. "Hanna? Um...are you okay? I mean..."

It's posted. They all know. Hanna steps into her room and closes the door without even looking at Becky.

Someone sends the CBC the link to Jarrod's Facebook page. That afternoon, the president of the university is surprised at the front door of his home by a reporter and a cameraman. But by then, Jarrod has taken down his Facebook page. Just in case. And, besides, he has enough data.

The Board of Governors calls an emergency meeting.

Jarrod isn't worried. He's broken no laws, made no hate statements, harmed none of the six participants in any physical or intentional way. And didn't he voluntarily take down the Facebook page as soon as things started to get out of control?

Hanna is already packed. Her parents will be there in an hour to take her home.

Claire and Megan haven't said a word the whole time Hanna was talking. They couldn't. It seemed too unreal.

"Mom and Dad looked pretty worried when they got to my dorm. They already heard a bit on the radio about what was going on. I just told them I was quitting because who'd

want to go to a university where stuff like that happens."
Hanna looks from Megan to Claire.

"You didn't do anything wrong, Hanna," says Claire, softly. "Not one single thing."

Megan can picture Hanna sitting in class like that, just waiting for someone to post a photo of *H*. Because, for sure she'd know someone would eventually do it. She'd feel so awful. And scared. "Maybe if you told the police..."

"What could they do? Jarrod didn't break any actual laws."

"That's stupid," says Megan. "He's a psycho!"

"I really got messed up by him. The whole time I just thought he was like this ordinary normal nice guy. I actually thought we could be, like, boyfriend girlfriend."

"Anyone would think that," says Claire. "I mean, you went out with him a bunch of times and everything was okay."

"I should've at least had a clue about what was going on. I felt so stupid."

"No way he should get away with what he did," says Megan.

"A lot of people thought it was, like, this big joke. A bunch of frosh losers getting sucked in because they don't know anything about anything. It was humiliating. Really, really humiliating."

Hanna takes a deep breath and sighs. "Just when I think I'm done with that crap, I start getting crazy texts from Mrs. Gallo."

And then they get to Pinawa and Lloyd shows up. She knows it's all connected. Jarrod and Mrs. Gallo and Lloyd. Starting with Jarrod. And ending with Lloyd.

Chapter Eight

At Hope, they pick up the Trans-Canada again. Hanna is trying to concentrate on driving, following the yellow highway lines. She glances over at Megan. She's got her earbuds in, just looking out the window and listening to music. She hasn't said much today. Neither has Claire. Probably because of last night.

Claire sees that they're now driving beside the Fraser River. The last time they were by this river was near Mount Robson yesterday. She clicks on the map and follows the course of the river backward from Hope. All the twists and turns, like a ribbon blown by the wind. Sometimes like a pretzel. Even dividing in two and sliding around a place called Diamond Island, which looks more like a lemon than a diamond. North, north, north. Then east and south and east again and all the way back to Mount Robson.

She thinks of saying something about how it's kind of cool that they crossed this very same river and drove south while the river kept on going west and now here they're meeting up again a day later. Then she gets thinking of the white-water rafting guide explaining to everyone that the river they were on went all the way to the Arctic Ocean. But that was the Athabasca, not the Fraser.

Her mind's as twisted up as that river right now.

"That's the Fraser River," she says. "We were driving by it yesterday. Up by Mount Robson. And now here it is beside us again. All that way."

Megan doesn't hear her.

"Makes me think of the St. Lawrence River," says Hanna.

Claire wants to say the St. Lawrence isn't much like the Fraser River at all because it's just this straight line that starts at a lake and ends up in the Atlantic, and the Fraser is—

But she knows Hanna only said that to be nice. Instead of all of them being here in this car not saying anything when there's a ton of stuff they could be saying.

Afternoon traffic is streaming toward Vancouver. They just passed Abbotsford, still following the Trans-Canada signs west. Hanna is wishing she'd waited until Monday to tell them about Whitehorse and about how they'll be flying home without her. Right now, they could've all been in a great mood, finally this close to Vancouver. Driving into the city like crossing a finish line. *We made it!*

Claire is staring out across the blur of fence and fields toward the solid mountains. She's remembering watching a seagull rise from a rock ledge and fly out across a bay toward the horizon. It had been dusk, and the gray of the Atlantic had been the same gray of the clouds that blocked the sky. The gull had flown down close to the water and then up again, curving away from the shore toward the horizon. Soon, no matter how hard she tried to find the lift of wings or a swoop low against the water, there was nothing, even though she knew it was still out there somewhere, moving farther and farther away.

Megan is thinking about Hanna's plan. It's the surprise element that's really getting to her. After all the distance they traveled between home and here, after everything they did together and talked about and hoped for. After everything that happened. Realizing this was her plan all along.

Hanna is trying to ignore the guilty feeling that won't let go. Leaving is inevitable anyway. Even Megan must know that. Claire is so quiet. Maybe for her, because of Caleb, this feels like another loss.

She signals and merges into the slow lane, wishing there was some way she could switch the mood.

They're sharing the room at the hostel with two Chinese women, a daughter who looks about forty and her mother who might be seventy. They've already chosen bottom bunks. They can't speak English, which makes it even easier for Megan to basically not say much, like she's been doing all day. Claire and Hanna try a couple of awkward sentences, maybe a bit too loudly, but soon everyone gives up and just does a lot of smiling and nodding.

The women seem like very nice people. From what they've managed to say, Canada Place is highly recommended, and also a Chinese garden where maybe a doctor lives. The daughter shows them pictures she's taken there. It looks exactly like a garden in China, even the buildings and trees.

Claire finds the site for the Vancouver Aquarium and clicks on the penguin cam. Three or four penguins are swimming and splashing in the pool, and one is standing by itself on the side. "Penguins," she says, tilting her phone toward the two women.

"Penguins," they say, smiling.

"Cool," says Hanna.

Megan comes over to take a look.

"I think that little guy's afraid to jump in," says Claire. Now everyone's in a small huddle around the phone. "Oh! There he goes!"

"Too funny," says Hanna. "We'll definitely go see them tomorrow."

At the aquarium, Megan is acting like nothing's fun. Hanna has given up on hoping that will change, and Claire is just trying to keep things at least partly normal. After they see the penguins, they go to the Amazon exhibit and then do an Arctic Gallery tour.

It's almost two o'clock when they finally get to Third Beach.

Hanna's been thinking about the dimes all morning. Probably she should just keep them and not say anything. It really feels like a lame idea anyway, now that they already know what's happening tomorrow. But Claire would still think it was a fun thing to do. It could sort of cheer her up a bit.

She waits until they're just about to wade into the water. "I've got something for us," she says. "Here's yours, Claire. And...this one's Megan's, and this is mine."

"What's this for?" says Megan.

"Look at the year."

"Hey," says Claire. "Mine's when I was born."

"Birthday dimes," says Hanna. She decides not to say how long she's had them. "We can throw them in the water, sort of like a symbolic thing for driving all the way from the Atlantic to the Pacific. Make a wish."

"The *Bluenose* for Nova Scotia," says Claire. "Cool!"

"Here. Throw this one if you're so hyped about it." Megan drops the dime in Claire's hand and goes back to lie on her beach towel. Why give Hanna the satisfaction of even watching this whole stupid thing? Like whoopee. We made it to the Pacific Ocean. And, oh yeah, I forgot to tell you, I'm dumping you guys at the airport and taking off without you.

She doesn't even turn around when she hears Hanna shout, "One! Two! Three!"

At the airport, Megan still isn't talking much, which is making Claire tense up even more about where they are and why. She's determined not to cry.

Hanna checks them in. Vancouver to Montreal. Montreal to Halifax. "Between flights, you'll have time for something to eat. You can't buy stuff on the plane without a credit card, but you can get something before you board and take it with you if you want." She gives them their boarding passes. "Okay, then. You're all set." Her smile isn't real. "Come on. Sisters' group hug." She pulls them into a tight circle, their faces pressed together. "I'm really gonna miss you guys."

Tension is a boulder in Claire's chest. She takes a deep breath and holds it. *I'll miss you too. I'll miss you too.* But she can't say this out loud. If she does, her breath will escape and the boulder will tumble and crash.

"Text me." Hanna's eyes are brimming with tears.

"We have to go, Claire," says Megan. "Hanna has to get Charley's friend." She walks into the security area and stands in line, not looking back.

"Take care of Megan, Claire. All that who-cares stuff is fake. She wants us to think she's tough, but she isn't."

"I know."

"Will you do me a big favor when Mom and Dad get home?"

"What?"

"Talk up all the major pluses of Mom buying a new car. It could really save my ass."

They both laugh, which makes Claire want to cry even more.

"You better go see if Megan's getting searched for illegal possession. Here's a hug for Mom and Dad."

When Claire is in the line, she turns and waves. Hanna holds up her phone and gives a signal to text her.

The security guard points down the row of doors leading into the screening area. "Number 3, please."

She looks again for Hanna, but she's already walking away. If she stops and waves one last time, Claire wants to be standing there ready to wave back. But Hanna keeps on walking until she disappears into the crowd.

"Miss? Third door, please."

Claire goes through the security door and puts her backpack in a plastic tray on the conveyor belt. She takes off her sneakers and puts them in the tray too.

In the boarding lounge, she sees Megan standing at a window, looking out at the planes on the tarmac. She never did like flying. Claire watches her for a moment but doesn't go over to the window. She finds a seat and takes her book out of her backpack. Her eyes skim over the words on the page, but they have no meaning. She looks around at people in the departure lounge. How many are leaving home and how many are going back?

Her phone chimes. Bear! And he's got his own phone. What's with that? She sends him a quick *hi* back and says she's at the airport with Megan.

I know, he says.

She looks up and sees Megan texting someone. It takes her a split second to do the math: Bear.

Megan comes over and sits down, her phone still in her hand.

"Bear's got a phone," says Claire. She knows she's stating the obvious.

"Norma and Edgar got him one for painting the house." Megan scrolls past a couple of photos, then turns the phone toward Claire. "He finished the front."

"Hey. Wow. Looks great." Her phone chimes, and there's a picture of Jake—mostly just the dog's nose pressed against Bear's phone. "Check this! Too funny!"

"Don't think what you're thinking," says Megan.

"Am I thinking something?"

"We're friends. That's all."

"Friends is good. I get that."

Their phones chime, and they assume it's another picture from Bear. It isn't. It's Hanna: *I love you guys. That's what this whole trip was about. Not about leaving. Don't be mad. Don't be disappointed. xo xo*

Claire looks at Megan, then quickly texts back: *I love you too. Our trip was the most fun I ever had in my life.*

Megan is just sitting there, holding her phone.

"You can't stay mad forever."

"She just feels guilty." Megan gets up and walks back over to the window.

Claire sees her texting. Might be to Bear. But maybe not.

It's raining when they board the plane.

"You want the window seat?" says Megan.

"Don't you want it?"

"Doesn't matter."

As soon as they're in their seats, Megan starts scrolling through the movie choices. Tuning out.

"Did you text Hanna?" says Claire.

Megan looks impatient. "All I said was that if she loves us, she sure has a funny way of showing it."

"You have a funny way of showing it too."

A flight attendant goes past, closing overhead bins.

The plane slowly taxis into position. It begins to move down the runway, gradually increasing speed until it accelerates in a deafening roar and lifts off. Claire watches droplets of rain skid in crazy patterns across the windowpane.

Megan shuts her eyes and tightly grips the armrests. The plane banks sharply and Claire's arm falls heavily against hers, a comfort she can only admit to herself.

A chime finally sounds and the seat-belt sign turns off.

Megan tries to get lost in a movie, but she can't stop thinking about what Hanna has done. It's too much like all those times when they were little kids and she would take off with her friends and leave Megan behind, even though she was supposed to stay with her like their mother said. She would start crying and Hanna would turn around and shout at her to go home. It feels like she's four years old again. She hates feeling this childish.

Claire has convinced herself to stop stressing about

what's going on. She can't do anything to change it. Now, she's thinking about what she's going to do as soon as she gets back home. She'll go out to the lake and take the matted-up teddy bear with the small black eyes off the tree and bring it home and make a cozy place for it on her bed. It doesn't matter who thinks that's weird.

Hanna is on the Trans-Canada, driving to Cache Creek where she'll take the Caribou Highway and head north toward Whitehorse. Though Charley's friend Kendra is right there in the passenger seat beside her, the car seems really empty now. She glances over at cars in the opposite lane, going to Vancouver just like she and Claire and Megan were doing a few days ago. She tries to block the noise of the windshield wipers slamming back and forth and the traffic zooming past. Keeps listening for the sound of airplanes overhead.

Though they're not aware of it, they are all traveling in the same basic direction right now. Hanna following the highway as it curves back toward the Fraser River. Claire and Megan flying far above the dark clouds that hide the white-capped mountains.

All caught in the sudden distance between them.

Acknowledgments

It's an amazing experience to be published by Pajama Press, all keen professionals who've welcomed me into their circle. I appreciate their friendships and everything they do to help move my manuscript from its hopeful beginnings to a published novel. Gail Winskill and Ann Featherstone are always clear, fair, and insightful in their responses to my work. Thank you both so much.

I appreciate my partner Jim's constant calm, especially when deadlines keep me in my writing studio and inside my imagination beyond the hours I intended.

My sister Barb's enthusiasm for my writing doesn't waver. It sits here at my desk beside me, making sure any self-doubts can't creep too close.